JENNIFER ANTELL

Jenny Antell was born in Sherborne, Dorset and educated at the town's grammar school. She trained as a nurse in the 60's and went on to settle as a practice nurse for 29 years before returning to Sherborne after retirement.

She started writing seriously in 1995 and has since written 3 novels. The CUCKOO and the WREN is her third.

THE CUCKOO
AND THE WREN

A novella

JENNIFER ANTELL

Copyright © 2025 Jennifer Antell

The right of Jennifer Antell to be identified as author of this work has been asserted by her in accordance with the Copyright, Designs and Patents Act 1988.

All rights reserved.

The characters and events portrayed in this book are fictitious. Any similarity to real persons, living or dead, is coincidental and not intended by the author.

No part of this publication may be reproduced or transmitted in any form or by any means, electronic or mechanical, including photocopy, recording, or any information storage and retrieval system, without permission in writing from the publisher.

*To my late mother and father,
without whom this story would never have been written.*

THE CUCKOO
AND THE WREN

PART ONE

When I was a stick thin child hiding under a slippery eiderdown something in the Awful Attic would come down the Scary Stairs at night and stand outside my bedroom door. It started in nineteen forty-seven. I know it was then because Pa had not long come home from the war. I would lie in the bed that he made and listen as the floorboards creaked. That's why my heart is weak now. All that terror. And now, since my recent incarceration here, the haunting, if you want to call it that, has started again after all this time.

My father and my mother. Pa's initials were carved on the back of my headboard. They were also on the mahogany sideboard in the front room. That was a cumbersome and ugly thing; the beading had already fallen off by the time my mother died but I can see her polishing even now, frantic with her tin of Ronuk. I would watch her from the corner of the room and pick at my hair slides as I inhaled that cloying lavender smell.

'Let me,' says Ma and she drops the smelly old rag and waves her hands in front of me as I duck and whine.

'Don't.'

'You've got a long face. It looks better when I do it. Makes you pretty.'

'I don't want to be pretty,' and I shrug her off.

'You will one day.' She huffs as she picks up the cloth from the arm of the settee and starts rubbing at the sideboard again. It was all right for her with her big eyes, her bouncing hair and her rosy face.

In a few minutes she'll be in the parlour washing her hands and cooking up some stew or casserole or fish or liver while I bite my nails.

It's the same in this place. Some nights, whatever it is outside my room, breathes. It waits and I listen. The door is usually ajar but even so I've seen the handle move. I know it's not the night staff because they giggle and clatter about as they carry their trays of nonsense and push trolleys and wheelchairs up and down the corridor. Some are foreign, some are black. Sometimes I say, 'I can't understand what you're saying,' but they sigh and ignore me or raise their voices as if I'm deaf or stupid. Or they play with their mobile phones.

Nobody believes me but it's like history repeating itself.

'Liver and bacon today, Rosie. Your favourite.'

'It's not my favourite and you know it.'

The black one chuckles and plonks the plate in front of

me, ties a bib at the back of my neck and starts to cut the liver into bite sized pieces.

'I can cut it myself.'

'You'll have it all over the place.'

I'm trapped by her bulk as she messes about with my food.

'I like it,' says Janet.

'You like everythin', Darlin'. You so easy to please.'

'Teacher's pet,' I mutter.

'Oh, poo,' laughs Janet.

I mix the potato into the gravy and smell it first before I put it in my mouth. It smells of nothing. I call for the salt. I wouldn't put it past them to put something unthinkable in the mash and I watch as Janet chews a piece of bacon and pulls at a stringy bit, a long slither coming out of her mouth pale and fatty like ectoplasm.

I say, 'This is vile.'

'Rosie, you such a misery. Eat up. You need to keep strong.'

'In this place, I do. You're so right.'

She gathers dishes from another table, pushes at the swing doors with her backside and disappears into the kitchen, the doors thumping and swinging backwards and forwards allowing laughter and the crashing of pots and pans to escape.

'And where's my salt?' I shout after her. I want to go back to my room. I push the plate into the centre of the table. 'I need to lie down.'

Janet chomps away with her mouth full. 'If you go now

you'll miss the steamed jam sponge. And custard.'

'Huh.'

'Anyway there's no-one to take you back yet. They're busy. And Caroline is coming this afternoon to talk to us about music.'

'I want to lie down,' I say to nobody in particular. 'Where's my room?' The black one is back from the kitchen. 'Can you take me back to my room?'

'You so dissatisfied all the time, Rosie. 'I'll take you back when we've finished here.'

Her hand rests on my shoulder for two seconds. I reach up to touch it but it's gone. She's gone.

THE TIMES I remember lying in that bed, tucked in the corner across a fireplace that was never lit, just newspaper and kindling gathering dust. I can feel the springs, feel the dip in the mattress and the stone hot water bottle wrapped in one of Ma's old stockings and I can smell the fustiness of the silky blue eiderdown as I pull it up to my chin, even hear the drag of it against the blankets.

The space of the room is broken by the huge wardrobe and the chest of drawers with glass knobs; something else Pa made before I was born, before he went to the war.

It's outside my room again. I'm sure there was a tap on the door. I lie still and stop breathing, moving my eyes without turning my head. There's nothing to see other than furniture shadows but the door is open just wide enough for fingers to come through, fingers with jagged and dirty nails, then a hand perhaps and something terrible could slip into my . . .

There's another tap. Tap tap.

'Wake up, Rosie.'

A voice. 'She's dropped off, Didi'.

It's Janet. I'm not asleep, just resting my eyes.

The black one, Didi. She comes over with the wheelchair. I could walk if they were prepared to help, if they were to let me hold on. But they always have something else to do that's more important. In fact it's not a real wheelchair it's one of those with a hole in the seat and suddenly I'm on the lav with my knickers down and the door open.

'How do you expect me to go when anyone might come in?'

'It's your room, Rosie and it's private. I'll close the door. Just have a pee. '

'Don't close it all the way,' I call.

But she's gone again.

One stormy day when I was in my room and the window was left open a little (and I can open it myself if I feel strong enough) I could hear the sea and if those women had stopped their clattering outside my door I would have heard seagulls.

I listen now.

The waves must be high; they're dragging at the pebbles. That constant, terrifying sound. Crashing and dragging. Crashing and dragging. Crashing and . . .

'What you still doin' on that toilet, my God? Come on.

I'll clean you up and get you into bed. Ola!' she yells and it shoots right into my ear.

A hand circles my other arm. It must be Ola. And I'm pulled up from the seat and wiped.

'I lived near the sea when I was a child,' I say as Ola now fusses over my pillows.

The black one says, 'In you get, Girl and have a rest. We'll get you up when Caroline comes.' She helps me balance on the side of the bed, lifts my legs and swings me round. I flop back like a bag of bones as they pull off their rubber gloves and throw them in the bin.

MA SAID THAT I didn't have to go to school that day so I put on my mac and wellies and opened the back door.

'Can I go to the cove?'

She said, 'Don't be long. There might be a surprise later.'

But the draw of the ocean was greater than my curiosity and I skipped along the rough path down towards the sea.

It was a damp day but warm for February, Ma said, and a mist hovered over the offshore reef. There was no wind and everything was calm. The small waves tipped onto the beach in regular ripples leaving the spume behind. I liked staring out to the horizon. Just being there with the smell of salt and seaweed and the shrieking of gulls was enough for me as I breathed in and out.

I hear a man's voice, eerie, calling my name from far away. I turn and scramble up the bank, scrabble under the barbed wire, fight the gorse and climb into the field. I see a man coming through the five bar gate ahead. Ma is there too but holding back. He stands, watching and waiting, wringing his cap like Ma wrings her hands. I don't realise it straight away; I suppose it's because I've never seen him before but as I get closer I think, It must be Pa! And we walk towards each other, both very slow.

Eventually I can see that his hands are very big. Ma always said he had big hands. I sense it's him. It must be him.

It's Pa.

Ma comes through the gate then. She's put on her red cardigan. I can see it flashing its colour under her open coat. And she's taken out her curlers. Then I'm feeling Pa's khaki trousers on his thin legs, rough and smelling of damp as he pulls me to him.

Ma had always said he would be home one day but I didn't understand then, about the war. About cruelty and killing. Or dying. Or grieving. Or guilt.

He lets me go and turns to Ma slipping his hands onto her waist under her cardigan and I watch as he pulls her close. Her body arches as his arm forces her against him and her head falls back. But she's smiling up at him, her brown hair bouncing. He bends down and kisses the top of her head and then her mouth . . .

How lucky am I to remember that?

'What you smiling at, Rosie?'

'Oh. My father was very tall.'

'Uh, huh.'

'But I only once saw him kiss my mother.'

'But you here, Darlin. He must have done lots of kissin'

at some point.'

She and Ola chuckle together.

'What was his name?' asks Ola. She stands by the door, eager to get on with her work but kind enough not to rush.

'I'll have to think about that one.'

They laugh at the silliest things.

I desperately want to close my eyes. I hear the black one whisper, 'She very tired. Let her go to sleep now.'

'Sleep tight.'

They shuffle to the door.

'His name was Frank.' Or was it . . ?

SOME EVENINGS PA would take me walking. He would lift his cap off the peg and flip it on, leaving Ma to wash up and we would shut the gate, cross the road and walk down the long lane, cut through the hedge and field and drop down through a dip in the bank of grasses and gorse, brambles and barbed wire, to reach the cove.

To most, it wasn't beautiful.

Even at high tide there is a ring of seaweed where the pebbles make a ridge. The salty, fish smell of it is strong and we watch as more of it is pushed up onto the shingle and left there, limp like shiny brown rags: thong weed and bladder wrack, sugar kelp and wire weed. We crunch to the water's edge and shiver as the wind blows our hair, leaving the salt taste on our lips. I lick mine and question Pa. He says the air is full of salt. We stand as thin streaks of yellows and watery blues mix with greys above the horizon. We watch until the colours fade and the silver speckles that are dancing on the water disappear and darkness begins to roll in as the day ends.

Sometimes he holds my hand.

When I've got the courage, I'll get out of this bed, pull that door wide and confront it. Last night it opened three inches and if the night nurse hadn't come along just then and peeped inside who knows what might have happened. She insisted that the door had not moved but even so she stayed and brushed my hair until I lay down and settled.

She smoothed my cheek, muttered in some weird language and looked at me the way Ma used to when we were alone, smiling with her head on one side. I didn't understand what she was saying but it sounded nice.

'Are you Polish?'

'No, no, I am Romanian.'

'You must miss your home.'

'No, no, I am happy. I live in England now. Many of my friends have gone back to Romania but I love it here.'

'Always so many different nurses. I can't remember your names. Except Ola's.'

'Ola works in the day only. But there's Trish, Jennifer, Didi, Lottie.'

'My nights are always interrupted.'

'We wake you up?'

'Something comes and stands outside my door.' I almost whisper it.

'You have nightmares. I had nightmares as a child in Bucharest. I was scared of ghosts.'

'It isn't nightmares. I'm awake or have been woken and it knocks my door.'

'Why don't you say, "Come in?" '

She thinks it's amusing.

'What? You must be mad. Who knows what's out there?'

'I don't think you should worry, Rosie.' She gets up from her chair and stretches. 'I must go; others need me also.' She opens the door wide. 'You see, there is nothing. Shall I leave it open?'

'Just a little. Don't shut me in. Are you Polish?'

'Romanian.' She smiles and quietly leaves.

They must think I'm a fool. But I know what I know. It's come back after all these years. I can't imagine I will escape from it now.

MA AND PA are in the parlour sitting in front of the fire. The flames are bright orange with reds and purples licking at the chimney. Pa looks asleep. His head is right back on a flat cushion and his mouth is open. Sometimes his body twitches and he mutters under his breath as I stare at his thinness. Ma turns and watches me as I hover by the stairs in my nighty. My toes peep out beneath the hem.

'Up to bed, Rosie,' she whispers. 'I'll come in a minute.'

'Will Pa be going away again?'

'No.' She hesitates. 'He'll always be with us now.'

I feel I could burst with happiness.

Lottie comes into my room and stands close. I know her name is Lottie because she has a name badge on her uniform that I can read without my glasses. I've seen her before, I think.

'Morning, Sweetie.' She puts a mug of something that looks like tea on my locker and helps me to sit up.

'Sleep well?'

'I've had some bad dreams.'

'Oh, that's disappointing. But hopefully they will improve.'

I think about that.

Then I look at her face.

'You've been crying.' Her eyes are swollen behind her glasses and her nose is red and shiny.

'It's okay. Only a family tiff. My husband has a short fuse. Were you married?'

'I don't think so . . .' I look around for a photograph but there isn't one. 'I remember crying. Maybe all men do that. My father did the same. Used to see Ma red eyed.'

She's getting my dressing gown from the back of the easy chair and looking for the arm holes.

'Where are we going?'

'I'm taking you to the toilet and then a little wash and tidy before breakfast. But drink your tea first.'

'Sometimes I only remember the bad times but if I try hard I can remember when I was happy.'

'And when were you happy, Rosie?'

'When was I happy? Oh, the first time was when Pa

came home from the war. But my friend, Margaret . . . Her Pa didn't come home.'

EVERYONE WAS LAUGHING and running about being silly. I could see she wanted to join in but she stood alone in the playground. One by one we stopped running about and stared at her.

Roger Aplin said, 'Is your dad dead?'

There was a hush like there was a hole in the air.

'I think so. Mum says so.'

Ian Penny said, 'That's bad.'

'I don't think I've ever seen him.'

'So, that's okay, then.'

Margaret shrugged and she joined us and we all ran about again.

'And what was the second time? That you were happy.'

She's blowing her nose into a tissue.

'When I met Michael.'

'Was he your first love?'

'My only love, I think.'

She's struggling to get my arms into the dressing gown. Then someone comes in and helps her walk me to the toilet. I can manage it today but it takes forever.

Ah. My only love.

I try to remember but it's really hard because it causes my heart to turn over and my insides to shake. I want so much to . . . But he's not there; it's Pa in my head and he takes over.

He had a workshop, I know that much. He'd get up in

the morning and have porridge, then, when he had his apron on and his jacket and his raincoat if it was cold Ma would hand him a flask and a cheese sandwich in a bag and he would walk out of the back door into the weather. Sometimes, after school I would call in and see him. On his bench might be a piece of pale bare wood but most often it would be dark. He called it mahogany and he would plane it down, the shavings coming off in curls that drifted onto the floor. In the corner there was always a huge pile of sawdust and adding more to it stirred up its overpowering smell, making it linger, waiting for it to be carried home with him on his clothes along with the dust in his apron pockets and in his hair. It floated off him onto the lino or the mats at home and Ma would moan.

I kick at the sawdust and the shavings.

'Your ma will be cross, Rosie. 'It's filling your shoes.'

'What are you making?'

'A sewing cabinet. It's for cottons and scissors and . . . things.'

'Is it for me?'

'I'll make one for you when you're older. And I'll put a glass knob on the door and on the drawer. Just like this.'

'Why hasn't Ma got one?'

'I'll make one for her too, if she wants. But I have to make some money now.'

He continues to plane.

But why does the time that Pa came home from the war and we were happy to the time when the rot set in, seem so short?

THE ONE IN navy comes in with my laxative.

'Can I have something to help me sleep tonight?'

'But you have no trouble sleeping, Rosie,' she says.

'How do you know? I lie awake for hours watching that door.'

'Here, drink this down.'

'It could be poison. Besides you don't work all night so how do you know if I sleep or not?'

She sighs and takes a pen out of her top pocket, ready to scribble.

'If you don't take it you'll be constipated.'

'It's too sweet.'

'Rosie.' She drags my name through her teeth and I take the medicine and the other stuff.

There is shouting along the corridor and a door slams. It's not unusual; everyone speaks loudly these days trying to make themselves heard or attempting to, or just wanting attention. Nothing is ever done quietly and nobody ever tells me what's going on. They treat me as if I'm half witted.

THIS MORNING I woke with an uncomfortable feeling of despair. I've had it before many times when I've been left in the aura of a bad dream and I'm still in it when a young man swans in dragging on his rubber gloves. He's got a name thingy clipped onto the pocket of his tunic. It's Malcolm. His photo is on it. I think I've seen him before. I don't think he's been here long, like me and I'm sure he's usually clean shaven but today he's got bum fluff round his mouth and chin. Thinks he's handsome.

'Ah, Rosie,' he begins.

I'm tempted to respond with, Ah, Miss Cooper, but I don't because I'm still feeling upset and confused and they all use my Christian name here, anyway. But I quite like the look of him; he's so sure of himself. And swanky. I stare at his very green eyes.

'D'you think you can walk, with my help to the bathroom, now? Or shall I get the chair, Darlin'?'

It's his Irish accent that floors me.

'Are you putting me in the bath?' I'm on the verge of crying. Maybe he can see that. I feel I'm welling up, the tears coming right up from my throat and filling my head.

He sits on the edge of the bed and looks for my hand. 'Well, now', he whispers, 'what have I done to upset you this mornin'? Or is it just you bein' here in this place? It can be grim sometimes, I admit that but it can also be grand as well, you know, if you give it a chance.' He leans closer. 'Is it bathroom with the zimmer, then or with the chair?'

He has a lovely smile.

'Where are you from?'

He stands again and towers over me. 'County Kerry. But I also lived in Dublin for many years.'

'I think I wanted to go to Ireland. With Michael.'

'And who is Michael, then?'

The early dream hovers in my mind. I knew it was still there somewhere.

The picture of him. It comes back to me from the fog. First a glimpse in an old photograph. Then his backing away from me.

'Sure, Rosie, you're going and I know you have to leave. But you're makin' me sad.'

We're in a crowded room so I can only see and hear the bobbing heads talking, muttering, doing everything in their power to stop me hearing his voice. Then he's in the centre of the hubbub looking at me. He's not tall but for some reason his head is above the others. Then he waves, trying to attract my attention but I'm all attention and can only watch open mouthed as he drifts through the crowds backwards, like he's on wheels to the end of what appears now to be a great hall. He's waving, waving until he's so small I can't see him anymore, just his hand, waving.

I feel such despair. Such longing.

'So, is it bathroom with the chair and then breakfast with the zimmer?'

Eventually I say, 'Get the zimmer. I can walk to both. I'm not decrepit yet.'

'Andy is bringing his accordion this evening,' says Janet.

She's eating porridge; something else that's unbearable. She has a lump on her chin about to drop onto the tablecloth. I keep my eye on it as she shovels another spoonful into her lopsided mouth. Cornflakes is as much as I can manage but they've added a chopped banana

'Did I ask for this?'

'It's good for you, Girl. You gettin' skinny. Shrivellin' away.'

'We'll come in for breakfast one day, Didi, and she won't be here,' laughs Janet. 'She'll have disappeared completely.'

'Gone into spontaneous combustion.'

They chuckle together.

'I'll be dead, you mean,' I mutter. 'Bloody good job.'

'Oh, come on, Rosie,' says Janet. 'We're only messing around. Let's think of some tunes for Andy to play.'

All her yapping has caused the porridge on her chin to slide down and plop onto the table. She'll be lifting her useless hand there in a minute to steady her bowl and her dead fingers will slide right onto it.

'Bugger Andy,' I mutter but she doesn't hear because Didi is there wiping the dollop away.

As it turns out Michael is planning to ask Andy to play some Irish melodies.

'Thank you, Michael,' I say when he passes through to get the tea. His green eyes twinkle in my direction and I feel a mixture of joy and sorrow.

'It's Malcolm, Silly,' says Janet.

I'd like to give her a good slap.

ANDY PLAYS FOR us at supper time while we slop up soup and try to guess what's in our sandwiches. Then he carries on for just a while longer afterwards so that we can wind down after all that excitement. And mostly it does have a calming effect. But Janet is a bit down in the dumps this evening because hubby didn't come in today so I pipe up, Bring on the male stripper! And the place is in uproar for a second or two, mostly with objections but a few guffaws are in there somewhere. From the men, obviously. I look across the table and Janet gives me a weak smile. So does

Andy but he's eager to get off home, I can tell.

'And my last tune. I want you all to sing or hum along. So behave yourself, Rosie; this one is especially for you.'

He starts the tune with a gentleness that holds me; stringing out the notes and then adding his voice. *'Oh, Mary . . .'*

That's me. Rosemary. He's singing for me.

'. . . in the place where the dark Mourne reach down to the sea.'

Michael played this for me on his mouth organ, his warm wet lips sliding backwards and forwards, sucking and blowing so softly that sometimes I hardly heard it. I know the tune so well; the words don't matter. His hair flopped on his forehead and his hands cupped the instrument like he was caressing it. Like he caressed me. His rough fingers on my neck. His tongue on my neck.

'C'mere, Rosie, my love,' and his arms are around me in the cold alley as he lifts me off the ground and my body is against his all the way down, my coat open, his coat open. *'God, you're grand, so you are, I want to eat you up.'* His hands are then on me pulling me in. *'But you girls wear so much feckin' clothes. Preservin' your chastity. Puttin' me off.'*

'I don't want to put you off, Michael but my Aunty . . .'

'Bugger yer Aunty, Rosie, I want to love you . . . I want to love you . . . I want to love you . . .'

There's a hand on my hand and a whisper close to my ear.

'Here, Rosie, take it now,' and I turn and accept the tissue from Malcolm and dab my eyes.

'Music gets to you,' I say.
'It does, so.'

Those first years with Ma and Pa were . . . but there's no one left now to ask about that time.

Ola comes into my room when I'm in the easy chair trying to think. Her face is above mine when I open my eyes.

'Rosie, you have a visitor.'

'I don't know anyone.'

'Her name is Brenda. She says she's your cousin.'

'Brenda? When was the last time I saw her?'

'She's come with her daughter, Lorna. Shall I bring them in?'

'Has she come to gloat?'

'Rosie!'

I'm shuffled into an uprightish position and before I know it these visitors are hovering with flowers.

'Am I about to die?' I stare at the bouquet.

Ola says, 'Don't be silly, Rosie. I will find another chair and a vase and then make a pot of tea.' She looks at the wrinkled one. 'Sit down and be comfortable. Please.'

'It's been a long time, Rosie.'

'Has it?'

'And do you remember Lorna, my daughter?'

Ah, Lorna. There's something about that one . . .

'It's been a long time, Brenda.'

'I just said that.'

'So, what do you want? If it's about money, I haven't got any.'

'The money business is all sorted. Don't you remember? I'm here because I want to see how you are. We're both getting older.'

'Want to see if I'm any nearer to the pearly gates, I expect,' and I find that funny, probably because Lorna is trying not to laugh behind her hand but we end up laughing together. I attempt to be serious. 'Did I ever tell you about the haunting in the cottage? Can you remember when it started?'

Brenda looks confused in spite of her lofty look. Three years older than me. And a know all. And she's tarted up with lipstick and mascara, even now.

But I can't be bothered. 'Well, it never happened when you were staying with us, so I don't suppose I ever did.'

'Can't say I remember,' Brenda says.

'Sounds intriguing,' pipes up Lorna.

'Well, it happened then and it's happening now. Right here. Outside that door.'

'Didn't we have fun, though when I used to stay those hot summers?'

I think about it.

For three summers Brenda came to stay and the haunting stopped. We would talk together into the night, giggling. Are you asleep yet? No. Nighty-night, then. Nighty-night. Are you asleep yet? And we'd giggle again. Why do I think about her now with resentment when I can remember those early days with such fondness. They were long and hot and we could run to the cove and swim if the sea was calm because on a rough day I wasn't allowed; the sea was too deep, trapped by the offshore reef and it was dangerous, Pa said.

Eventually Brenda started shutting the bedroom door when she undressed at bedtime and she would drape a white cotton bra over the bottom of the put-you-up and stand in front of the mirror and gaze at her face. And when we were at the cove she would pin up her long curls with Kirby grips.

Her toes are at the water's edge. The soft breakers ripple and drag and we scream even though the water is warm and we run backwards over the sand shouting how the pebbles hurt our feet. The sky is a hazy blue with puffs of white clouds here and there. It's a perfect day and she squints as she looks at me because she's facing the sun.

She says . . .

'What was it you said, that day?'

'What day?'

'On the beach. That hot day. I got the sun.'

'We had many lovely days.'

Lorna puts her spoke in. 'I've got three children, Rosie and five grandchildren; the eldest is called Finn.'

Brenda says, 'He's my great grandson.'

'Must be second or third cousins,' says Lorna.

'Once removed, twice removed, three times a letter, four times something better.'

'That's sneezing, Rosie,' says Brenda.

'What are you talking about?'

'Once a wish, twice a kiss . . .'
'Want to see some photographs, Rosie?'
'I'd like to know what upset the applecart,' I say.
Ola comes in with tea on a tray.
'I've found you all some Angel cake.'

I'M TRYING TO make sense of it all but I'm bombarded with thoughts. And it's hard to remember sometimes; there's so much imbedded with fear and horror that I try not to think. Then it comes out at night and it's all about that door, about Brenda and her vile mother and sweet Margaret and Ma in the rain and Pa in a fury.

MA IS HANGING sheets on the line; they're flapping around her face in the wind and I can see that she's struggling. Her hair is in her eyes and she's dropping the pegs. I don't even think of helping her but I tell her that I don't want Brenda coming to stay any more. She doesn't stop what she's doing and turn to look at me like she used to.

She mutters, 'All right, then,' and she carries on pegging out the washing.

'ROSIE, WE'RE MOVING you into the television room.'

'I want to get into bed.'

'It's a special occasion. Remembrance Sunday tomorrow and we thought you might like to see the service from the Royal Albert Hall.'

The one in navy wheels me through my open doorway

into the corridor and down to the sitting room. I'm parked up next to - somebody. There's a military band and drumming.

'Oh, let me go to bed.'

'But wasn't your father in the war? I think you said he was.'

Michael comes in with the drinks trolley.

'We're late tonight lovely ladies and gents but, sure it's good to have a late one once in a while. You've all got your poppies? And who wants the drinking chocolate and who wants the Horlicks, now?'

WITH THE CURTAINS closed and the heating on it's hard to tell if it's summer or winter but with the Zimmer I can sometimes get out of bed myself and get to the window to check. I have to be sure that I do it as quickly as I can because someone is sure to come in and moan. But this is supposed to be my home, isn't it? Yet I can't do this and I can't do that.

I reach the window eventually and pull one of the curtains aside. There is nothing but darkness. I press my hand flat on the freezing glass and shuffle around with the Zimmer and use all my strength to push the sash window up. Breathing is difficult but eventually it gives and it rises about four inches as I lean into the window seat. A cold blast whistles in and catches me unawares making me cough. I listen and can hear the sea; it's a way off but it sounds like a forest blowing in a gale.

That particular night when I was young and innocent

and very scared it must have been like thunder because of the wind and rain.

I'M STILL AWAKE and I can hear Ma and Pa's raised voices downstairs. I don't know what they're saying but it makes me feel bad, makes my heart beat faster. It's Pa mostly. Ma never shouts. There's a crash and the shouting stops.

Pa is coming up the stairs, his feet heavy on the treads. His fist bangs against the wood panelling on the landing making me start then he goes into his room. I wait until I hear him fall into bed and then listen for Ma but she doesn't come. Behind the dividing wall the bed creaks as he turns over and I lie there forever until I'm sure that he must be asleep. I push the bedclothes back and step onto the lino. My toes curl with the cold. I don't think of the haunting as I venture to the door and go through.

I glance up the Scary Stairs then take small, quick steps along the landing past my parents' room. Pa is snoring already.

If Ma is down there I'll say I feel sick. And I do feel sick; it's the truth.

I SHIVER AND cough so I pull the window down and shift the Zimmer until I can struggle into bed. That was a stupid thing to do. Getting into bed is a mammoth task. I'm now uncomfortable, my pillows are all wrong and I lie there in a sweat, struggling to breathe.

Another thing. The other day I asked for blankets. This

duvet is too thin. On nights like this when the wind howls and the sky opens its floodgates I can lie in this bed and shiver. I watch the curtains billow because now a draught is coming in. Typically, no-one has brought me anything. And when was the last time one of them thought to help me with a bed jacket? Or give me an electric blanket? Or a hot water bottle, even?

The black one barges in.

'What you ringin' that bell for now, Rosie?' She fusses over the pillows and the duvet and tries her best to hoick me up the bed.

'I didn't.'

'You did, my girl.' She flips off a switch beside my bed. 'You got a problem?'

'There's something horrid somewhere.'

'Ha,' she laughs, softer now. 'You so right there.'

'I want the light left on.'

'You got the night light right here.' She points.

There's a dull glow

'But the sea is so rough tonight.'

She bends over me and lowers her voice. 'Honey, there ain't no sea round here. But if you say it's rough then it's rough. Now you settle.'

She bustles out the door.

I don't understand. It's a wild night outside.

JANET IS ON a roll because hubby has come in; seems to me that he tries to come on a regular basis. He fusses about, stroking her arm, whispering and laughing at nothing, until she pushes him off and they giggle like silly teenagers. Probably a filthy joke or something to do with sex. Men are like that. She's still attractive. Hair done when the hairdresser's here. Low lights. Must have money. He's in a cashmere jumper. Pink. Pa would never have worn pink. Nor Michael. Men wear whatever they like these days.

Michael comes over. He's wearing a pale blue tunic but you can't see what he's got on underneath. I can imagine, though. I think it might be a white T shirt. When he bends down to speak to Janet I can see a glimpse of it and of dark hair. Oh.

. . . my fingers in that chest hair, and in that fuzz on his belly just below his button and my hand too wary to go any further.

'Lie down with me, Rosie. C'mon. Let's just touch and play, now. Let's be horizontal.'

'Your Ma will come in,'

'No, she knows better than that. She was young once, you know.'

'But she's in the kitchen.'

The hatchway is between us and I can hear her messing around wondering what we're up to.

'We can put the cushions on the floor. C'mon.'

Oh, I want to. Oh, I want his hands on me. I take off my white blouse with the easy buttons and he stares at my cotton bra, at my skin. I think, if I don't do as he asks I'll lose him. But Ma's dead voice is in my ear and Aunty's voice overpowers it. He kisses me softly then harder and his kisses go to my chest and he's pushing at my bra until I get a thrill of being exposed to him and his kisses are on my breasts, my . . .

There's a knock at the hatch.

'Michael. Can I get you two a cuppa?'

I'm struggling to get my bra down and my blouse done up and he's saying, stifling a laugh, *'No thanks, Ma, we're grand here.'* And she goes away. But she might come back. Or come in the door. I can't have this fear.

What a fool. What a nonsense. What a time wasted.

Hubby is going home. His mouth is on hers and he has a tear in his eye when he pulls away. He makes it slowly to the doorway with a hobble and a backward glance. Janet waves with her good hand and smiles.

'He's a bit much sometimes. Don't you think?' she says, as I'm trying to keep awake but fascinated by their goings on; fascinated at how it makes me feel. Envious? Not of hubby, he doesn't appeal to me at all but it's his need of her. His caring, perhaps.

Malcolm is bringing Freda back from the toilet. She's in the Holy Chair. He's always leaning over the women, getting close to their ears, muttering sweet nothings. Brenda Lee . . . He could easily rub his lips on Freda's neck if he wanted too. I'm sure she'd like that. All the women would. Do any of these young things in uniform realise that even at this age I still get a longing?

But I'd be repulsive to him. Skin like paper, tough in places, blotchy, itchy, hair that needs a wash, bladder that is out of control, feet with nails like shells, thick and crusty.

Swollen legs squeezed with constricting stockings. But when I'm on my own in bed, under the duvet I can put my thin old mouth onto the soft fleshy part of my hand; that part on the back where it meets the thumb and I can pretend it's a kiss. Right now it could be anyone with a strong body and good looks, no matter if he wears glasses there's something sexy about a good looking man taking off his glasses to kiss you. Undoing that top button . . .

'Rosie, wake up.' It's Didi. 'You'll be complainin' tonight that you can't sleep again.' She plonks a hot chocolate on the low table beside me.

'I wanted Horlicks.'

'Sometimes, Rosie, you so contrary.'

'And you're snappy.'

'I worked all last night, if you want to know and worked most of today, too. We short on the staff and I can't help it if I want to go home to bed.'

'I want to go to bed.'

'And no getting' out and shufflin' to that window again. If it isn't the door it's the window.' She talks loud enough for everyone to hear as she walks off swinging her arms.

PA WAS A strong man but I never thought of them together, in bed. Ma was a pretty, softly spoken woman who rarely smiled but I suppose they made love. Everyone calls it sex now or that other word that seems to be used so freely these days. I sex, you sex, we sex. I think fuck is the only verb that really says it as it is; certainly can be used when there's no love involved. I'd like to think that Pa was a caring lover.

And Ma? I think she said once that after the war he changed.

That Brenda was a little tart. Staying one summer, smarming up to the boy on the beach and me like a gooseberry. Meeting him in secret at dusk but taking me with her so that I trailed behind, small thin thing that I was and holes in my cardigan. So much giggling.

'And where have you two been?' asks Ma.

'Out for a walk, Aunty, that's all.'

She's got that swingy way with her and I can see Ma doesn't like it. Pa is indifferent sitting in his chair, far away with the fairies, drifting off to sleep. Dozing, he says. But he wakes up in terror sometimes, sweating and moaning and Ma says,

'Don't mind your father. He had troubles in the war. He has bad memories. '

So he's like me in that way, but I know nothing about war.

'Wasn't he in a camp, Aunty?' asks Brenda.

That's new to me.

She's got to know everything, got to appear more knowledgeable than me.

'He was, Brenda but he doesn't like talking about it so keep it to yourself.'

'But Mum knows, doesn't she? And Aunty Vi?'

'I suppose.'

'Mmm.'

She's a sly thing.

'Michael.'

I call him as he passes my room and I cough; haven't had my inhaler yet. I suspect they're all behind again.

'Rosie. Or shall I call you, Rosemary?'

'Rosie is okay.'

He's squatted by my chair. 'I think you call me Michael on purpose, now, just to get Janet wound up.'

'Do I?'

He grins. 'So what can I do for you today? Hurry up, now, there's a good girl. I've a load to do.'

'When you go shopping will you buy me a lippy? Pink. Don't want to look like I've got a mouth like a red letterbox. Something subtle.'

'Now, why ask me, Darlin? I'm a bloke, now. Ola or one of the other girls would know more about that stuff than me.'

'They'll laugh at me.'

'I'm sure they won't.' He's ready to go already.

I give him my sweetest smile.

Someone calls out. 'Malcolm!' It's the one in navy.

'She's comin' round with the meds now, Rosie. He whispers, 'I'll see what I can do.'

'Ah, Malcolm,' she says when she's at my door, 'would you help Ola with Freda, please? Bit of a problem.'

Messed herself again, no doubt.

There's an emptiness in the room every time he leaves.

'Rosie. I've got your meds.' She rummages around in her trolley thing. 'Didi tells me you were out of bed last night. No wonder you couldn't breathe. But I'll talk to Dr

Pearce as soon as I can. He might want to examine you or prescribe some different medication. Oxygen might be – '

'I don't want to be lugging one of those things around all the time.'

'You won't be. It would be small and convenient. Handy for when you go out.'

'When am I likely to do that? Haven't got anyone to take me, anyway.'

'What about your cousin that visited you the other day? Her daughter said she'd bring her again.'

She hands me the tiny paper cup with tablets at the bottom. I shake them about. 'I have no idea what these things are for,' I say, but I down them in one with a glass of water.

'I've told you before, Rosie but I'm happy to tell you again if you'd like but I'm rather tied up right now.

'I know I have something for the old waterworks but do they make me go or do they try and control it? Whatever, none of it seems to make any difference.'

She's out the door before she hears that last bit.

I HAD TO go and live at Brenda's. I was sitting on the stairs. Thick carpet. Olive green. She had a school friend over. Aunty Bet was in the kitchen at the back of the house; it was so similar to Margaret's house in our village that it seemed I was transported back there and for a brief moment I was happy. Just for a few seconds I could have gone out of that front door and up the wet and windy lane and in at her house. And Ma might be there, clutching a cup, turning her head towards me and smiling.

I want to wee so badly that I can't get off the stair. Brenda and the other one have gone off somewhere, doing their hair or writing letters to boys. I think I have to ask permission to use the lav. There's a warm and cosy bathroom upstairs and another toilet downstairs. Oh, I need to go. I wriggle around. If only someone would come. I want to be at home but only Pa is there, mooching about with all his thoughts. And the lav there is outside with a latch. I can't get inside. It's stuck behind a pile of snow that's getting higher all the time. I've shouted to Pa but he ignores me; he's too busy shovelling it from the back door. If I can't get in there I will have an accident through my knickers and down my legs all warm and wet and the snow will be yellow and mushy and Pa will shout and . . .

'Rosie, Rosie. Never mind, now, we can soon fix you up.'

'It's not nice.'

'We can give you a wee pad. It's not a problem.'

'Well, it is to me.'

'Sure, but it happens.'

What can be worse than wetting the bed in front of a man? In front of Malcolm, no less. He sits me in the chair, takes off my nighty and cleans me up with warm water and a cloth. Now he can see my scrawny body and my parts. Then there's my dressing gown and he puts it around my shoulders as he strips the bed. Oh, I do love him.

'Stay there, Darlin'. I'll get you dressed; it's time to get up now anyway. And I've got the nice 'Old Rose' pink lippy you were hankerin' after. And we'll do your hair and you can put the lippy on and look wonderful.'

Oh, Michael, I do so love you.

THERE'S A NEW one that's appeared on the scene all bossy and bright and wanting to organise everybody. She switches channels on the TV.

'I was watching that!' I'm fuming.

'They want, "Only Fools and Horses."'

'Well, I don't and I was watching that.'

'People don't want westerns any more, Dear.'

'Don't "Dear", me.' You don't even know my name.'

'It's Rosie,' shouts What's-His-Name. 'She's a grump. '

'Oh, we don't like grumps, do we ladies and gentlemen?'

'Who are you to come in and change channels, anyway?' I say through the mumbles and grumbles.

'Haven't you got a telly in your room, Rosie?' says the man. He's always coughing or blowing his nose and thrashing his handkerchief all over the place.

'No.'

'Why don't you get one, then? '

'I haven't got money to throw around. This place is using up what I have so fast it'll be gone before I'm dead.' But I'm almost dead now so it doesn't matter, I suppose.

I loved the cowboys. The big hats and handsome faces. The romance. The broken hearts. Wounded cowboys, lonely cowboys, needing love from me. Them needing me amid all the dust and heat. Until Michael came along.

The new one is wearing navy blue like she's flashing it around. And a shiny silver buckle.

'If I'm not allowed to watch it I'll go to bed.'

'Ola will help you as soon as she's free.'

This is what it's like, what it's going to be all the time, from now on. Sitting . . .

PA IS IN his armchair, shaking fag ash over the mat while Ma pokes the fire. His face lacks expression, his skin tough and lined.

'I'm throwing some onions in the fire,' she says, and in they go in shiny foil. In an hour she'll poke them out and we'll eat the yellowed flesh oozing with butter. Pa's will be gone in seconds. He eats fast, says little and Ma lets out a sigh that says she's tired so I must go to bed early and there's me thinking it was going to be fun when he came home.

Or after, when it's too dark to see by the firelight alone and Ma puts a light on and I change into my nighty at last, I'm pleased to crawl into my bed and shove the bottle down.

THE TV IS too loud and what with the roar of laughter from the others and the blaring from the box I find it hard to concentrate. We didn't have a television. But Ma listened to the wireless in the kitchen when she'd finished cleaning the house and washing the sheets and pegging them out and boiling cabbage and potatoes and taking out her curlers.

Pa puts on his filthy, working apron with the huge front pocket, then his brown overall that's barely warm enough and then a tweedy jacket with broken pockets but good enough to ram his bag of bread and cheese in. He pecks Ma on the lips but it doesn't last long. He pats my head, opens the latch on the back door and he's off down the garden path to the road.

'What're you looking at?' she smiles.

'Why is he always so quiet? I thought he was going to be fun.'

'He has a lot going on in his head.'

'Because of the war?'

'Mostly. He was treated badly.'

'Will he get better?'

'I expect so. As time goes on.'

'I have things in my head.'

'So have I. Everybody has.'

But she doesn't want to talk about that so I keep my mouth shut for a while.

'So we must be kind?'

'Yes.'

'Margaret's Pa was killed in the war, wasn't he?'

'Yes. Now get yourself ready for school. I've got a busy day.'

She doesn't want to talk about that either.

SOMETIMES I THINK I get mixed up between fantasy and reality. Especially when I'm tired. So, did it happen that way? When Margaret and I went to the cove after school and Pa came to fetch us after work? We had our coats on but it was cold in the wind. I had a bobble hat and Margaret wrapped her scarf around her head. I was so glad that she wasn't miserable but she said that her mother was. She said her ma was trying very hard to get over it.

'Get over what?' I say, without really thinking.

'My dad being killed.'

'Oh.'

'I think about it sometimes, how it might have happened. Like, if he was shot or was he blown up?'

'Oh.'

'Or maybe he was left alone and it took days for him to die.'

I spend time dwelling on all this.

'I sleep in with Mum lots of the time,' she says. 'It's cosy.'

The waves are high and we feel blown about. Seagulls shriek all around, swooping and diving like they do. Their undersides and wings almost shine when the sun slides through the cold grey clouds to light up their feathers.

'Pa doesn't say much but we try to include him, try and be kind. Roger Aplin said that he was probably tortured in the camp.'

'What camp?'

'The Nips had camps for prisoners of war. That's what Roger said.'

'The Nips?'

'Japanese.'

We are as close to the sea edge as we can possibly get and

we turn over the pebbles and throw the seaweed about.

Margaret says, 'So, he was starved, most like, then?'

'Must have been.'

Smelling the seaweed can't be a fantasy. Remembering that conversation can't be a fantasy.

Is Margaret still alive? How I'd like to see her.

My feet are wet; it's got into my wellies.

I say, 'You could stay for tea if you want?'

'Here's your Dad.'

'Pa,' I shout and wave.'

Then he's with us laughing and smiling for once and larking about and we're shrieking like the gulls and roaring like the waves.

It's easy to be kind when you're happy.

THIS MORNING I feel a sense of dread and I'm wondering if it's a follow on from a dream last night. Or perhaps I have reason to be in a dread. It's the door. Of course. Whatever it is, it's waiting its time. I try to remember all the stuff clogging my head. I want to sift out the rubbish from the hard core, the wheat from the chaff. If I were to have a nice dream I'd be saying, Wrap your arms around me, Michael and kiss me. Kiss my skinny body.

He gets my glasses from the bedside table and puts them on my nose, makes sure they sit on properly. He checks behind my ears. Then he bends low and points to his name badge. It's Malcolm. Oh, kiss me dear Malcolm, I long for a kiss.

He pecks my forehead

But it's my lips that are left wanting.

'You must have been a real stunner, Rosie,' he says. 'Tell me about Michael while I take you for a wee.'

He manoeuvres me onto the Holy Chair with ease, his arms clasping me under my arms and around to my back. He can lift me like a puppet and I can hold him.

'Sure, I'm going to spray some of that expensive perfume on you when we're done, Rosie.'

'It's cheap rubbish and I think you're saying that because I smell of piss.'

'You're not one to mess around, now with fancy words, are ye?' And he laughs as he pushes me over the toilet hole.

'I met Michael at a gathering. Too few people to call it a party. I think I was sixteen? Seventeen?

'Young and beautiful.'

I snort because I was never beautiful but even so Michael waits for me outside the lav in the outhouse at his place along with the dust and the spiders and I'm still pulling my dress down. But he looks at me like there's no one else and the kiss comes naturally. It's my first kiss oh so lovely so warm and wet and the closeness of his face and the touch of his hands and my body against his. Oh, the memory. *And where did you learn to kiss like that, Rosemary?* as if I am used to it and he is just another one. But I think, he is the one who is used to it and it's me that is just another one. Then he goes into the lav. So maybe he didn't wait for me on purpose after all.

'And did you fall in love there and then?

I have to flop a flannel around my face and hands.

'Well, he came knocking on Auntie Bet's door asking for me. I'm sure I must have.'

Then Malcolm pushes me to the dressing table and brushes my hair and applies the lippy and the perfume.

'All ready, now, Rosie? Ready to charm Arthur? I think he fancies you.'

'Oh, God forbid.' And we both laugh.

'I could love you, Malcolm.'

But he pats my shoulder and I'm plonked next to Janet at the breakfast table, all my lovely thoughts drifting away with the steam from the teapots and the smell of Janet's scrambled egg until even the fragrance of my perfume has disappeared.

SOMEONE HAS BROUGHT in a cat. We're all expected to stroke it. It's calming, said the one without a uniform. Well, it doesn't calm me. In fact it horrifies me. My heart starts to beat like a Gatling gun.

'Don't bring it near me.' There's a nightmare rising up from the depths making me shiver and sweat at the same time.

'But she's beautiful, Rosie. So soft. Give her a stroke. Come on. Just one stroke.'

Arthur coughs like he's on the Woodbines and he's going to flake out any minute. It makes the cat struggle in the woman's arms.

'See, I knew she wouldn't want to get near her,' he says. 'She's a misery of the highest order. Lipstick and perfume. Done up like a dog's dinner. You won't get round me.'

I think the woman with the cat is called Caroline. She's the one who plans our entertainment but being here with all these dopes and the half dead is entertainment enough for me. I say to her, 'Can you bring me in a big photograph or poster of Clint Eastwood, Caroline? Please. In his cowboy hat. And with the cigar.'

Janet laughs and Arthur huffs.

'I want it on my bedroom wall and then I can look at him when I'm dropping off to sleep and it might give me nice dreams.'

Caroline says she'll see what she can do. She thinks it's a good idea and that shuts those two up.

The cat sweeps round my legs and purrs and I'm back there, in the back of my mind. I knew it would happen at some point. I knew that memory would come back and there it is hanging around in my frontal lobe. There are some things I can't remember and some things I don't want to remember. I know that much. But the pictures in my head now are so clear I can't stop them coming. Oh . . .

Pa comes in from the pub. He hooks his cap on the peg inside the back door and looks around the parlour. 'Where's your Ma?' he says.

I'm sitting with crossed legs on the mat in front of the fire and he's at the door holding onto the edge, trying to balance. Pretty is on the cushion in the big chair with her two kittens, feeding. The black one is in my lap. He can have his milk in a minute.

'She's upstairs.'

'Don't go thinking you can keep it.' He flops into the

other chair.

'But he's a little one.'

'It'll grow.'

Ma comes in from the stairs and pulls the curtain across. 'You're late.'

'Don't start.'

'I wanted you here earlier to do that job. It's gone on too long and now it's dark.'

'I'll do it tomorrow.'

He's lighting his fag; whipping his big hand backwards and forwards to put out the match. He's looking at me.

Ma goes to the sink under the window and holds on.

'Rosie,' she says, 'it's time for bed.'

'And why's she up so late?'

'She wants to play with the kitten.'

'She'll be getting used to it. She'll be loving it.'

'She already loves it.'

'I'll do it tomorrow.'

'You always leave it too late. Their eyes will . . .'

'Right!' And he's angry. It doesn't take much. He squeezes his fag down into the ash tray, pushes himself out of the chair and pulls the two kittens off their mother's teats with one hand, opens the back door to a certain angle and whacks their heads on the edge. Crack and crack and he's outside in the shed looking for a shovel or a spade and I get up and can see him within the light from the window throw them on the dirt while he digs a hole in the semi dark.

Ma is screaming. 'You could have waited until she's in

bed. You animal.'

He's inside again and grabbing my kitten from my arms and whacking him like the others. Outside he throws all three into the hole and my hand is at my mouth and I'm rigid as he slices the spade into the kittens in their grave.

Then Ma and Pa are both shouting and Pa is washing his hands and Ma is wringing hers and I'm standing there like a stick with only my eyes moving. Blinking. Then I'm throwing the curtain aside and I'm off up those stairs like lightning and under the blankets before Ma can make it to my bedroom trying to make excuses and crying. But I'm not crying. I'm too filled with horror to cry.

SOMETIMES, WHEN THE days are fine and Ola and the other one are in high spirits I start to wonder if it's all my imagination. Outside the sky might be brilliant blue and they might tell me I can go out on the patio for a few hours. Then, with the warm breeze drifting round me and a cup of strong tea I can believe how lucky I am and I start to think I might be a dreamer. Pa said I had nightmares. Once, after Ma died he said it was understandable.

'THERE'S NOTHING UP there,' said Brenda as we stood at the bottom of the Scary Stairs.

'Well, I know there is.'

'C'mon. I'll be with you.'

'No. And anyway Ma said not to go up.'

'Don't be silly.' She was up there like a shot, her daps

slapping on the wood until she rounded the curve near the top and her voice echoed down.

'C'mon, Softie. There's nothing here.'

I was so reluctant to go but I ventured each step dead quiet in case Ma heard and eventually we were both in the attic shuffling round in the dust.

'Well, it never comes down when you're here, anyway.'

'You dream it, Rosie,' and she peered out of the high window. 'How would it come and go? I think when you're older you'll realise it was only nightmares.'

Know All.

THE NEW ONE in navy comes into my room.

'Tonight, Rosie you'll sleep well. Lottie is on duty and she'll keep her eye on you.'

'And the door? Have they told you about the door?'

'I know everything, Dear. All the staff communicate.'

'You think I make it up. One of these days someone will believe me.'

'I think you need to close the door at night.'

I can't be bothered to argue. I'll just ask someone else to open it; Lottie, perhaps. She knows I don't like being shut in.

She drifts out the door in her tiny heeled flat black shoes like she's floating. Dear this and Dear that.

This room is reasonably cosy but it could be plush if they were to freshen it up. Fitted carpet and a comfy chair, but all tired. My room at home was cold with thin curtains that didn't shut properly and the old fireplace with the black grate that was never lit and my lumpy mattress. Silky blue eiderdown full of old feathers. Sheets sewn with sides to middle. And that walk on lino to the door.

So who's paying for all this worn beige carpet and heavy curtains and a door that was once glossy white and a chair with old cushions?

In the corridor the nurses walk up and down. I'm always one of the first to come to bed. I'm always ready. But they insist on propping me up now. Easier to breathe, Rosie.

After Ma died and I stayed at Margaret's we shared a room. It had flowered wallpaper and an armchair in the corner. And there was no attic to fear. I loved Margaret and her mother, whatever her name was. Gertie? Gracie. Ma and she were friends – at least for a while. But then it was like cats were let out of bags or some such horrible thing. Or stable doors were shut after horses had bolted. Something happened and I can't remember why. But no-one could separate Margaret and me. And her Ma still brought us treats in bed; cocoa and bread and cheese and we'd take a tiny bit of cheese and wrap it tight in a piece of bread till it was hard and depending on the state of our fingers, till it was grey. Then we ate them while we laughed.

'Why don't you see your cousin anymore, Rosie?' she asked one day.

'She told lies and all she wanted were boys and stuff.'

'What stuff? And what lies?'

'And she laughed at me.'

But I do remember. Somewhere.

And if she visits me again. I'll ask her outright.

Lottie comes in to kiss me goodnight. I know it's Lottie because she has outrageous glasses. She kisses everyone who's still awake. So I ask, 'Who pays for me staying here?'

'Can't answer that one, Rosie. You'll have to ask Sister.'

'What, that pasty faced one with a buckle like a dinner plate?'

She snorts with laughter, 'Yes, that one. Or Jennifer. Do you really not know or have you just forgotten?' She sits on my bed and takes my hand. 'Are you happy here?'

'I suppose I am but they're a load of deadbeats out there.'

'I think you put it on.'

'What?'

'All that grumpiness.'

'Some of them need a firework up their arse.' She has a sweet face when she smiles. 'Is hubby behaving?' I ask remembering what she told me.

'He has his moments.' She gets up to leave.

I don't know whether that's good or bad.

'Leave the door ajar, Sweetie,' I say.

She does it just how I like it.

Now I can keep an eye on it all night.

Roger Aplin had a newspaper and he brought it to school. He hid in corners with his friends making unnecessary noises over its contents.

Margaret comes over and says, 'Don't look at it Rosie,

it's horrible.' But her saying that makes me go and look over their shoulders and see the black and white photographs of horror.

'They'll have done this to your dad, Rosie. See?' says Roger. 'No wonder he's a weirdo.'

'Is he mental?' asks Ian Penny.

The paper is getting ripped and the boys are throwing pages around so I gather them up and fold them.

At home I ask Ma about what happened to Pa in the war because I can tell he's not right even though he's the only Pa I've ever known and sometimes he can be kind.

Ma rubs her fingers across her forehead and her lip quivers. I think she's going to cry. 'You don't have to believe everything they say in that paper.'

'But is it because of what the Nips did in the war?'

'Most like, Rosie,' and she flops into the armchair by the fire. 'But you're far too young to understand. When you're older . . .'

'Margaret's pa wasn't in a camp,' I say.

'No, but he . . .'

'Died. That must be worse then.'

'Possibly.'

'For Margaret's ma at least. Margaret never knew him, though, so it doesn't matter to her, really.'

Ma has become very breathy and she wipes a hanky over her eyes which are half closed and I'm suddenly aware that I need to stop talking.

I leave the torn paper's pages on the table and melt away into the shadows like I'm used to doing.

MALCOLM CREEPS INTO my room and my eyes are wide open. They get sticky so I'm rubbing them when he looks down at me and I know I must look pale and wrinkly.

'Lottie says to ask you if you slept well?' he says.

I have to think. 'Well, nothing came through the door.'

'That's a positive then. I'll go tell her.'

He leaves as quickly as he came in.

THEY TELL ME that Brenda is visiting this afternoon. I think I might confront her. I think she's filled with guilt. She wants to make amends. Well, I think Pandora's box has been opened and I know what it's all about; it's just been buried in my head somewhere with all the other stuff. If we talk then it'll all come rushing back about the cupboard under the stairs. There, that's a place I didn't want to recall, but it just popped into my head. I wish it would pop out again.

Michael helps me to 'freshen up'.

'C'mon, Rosie, I'll lather the cloth and you can wash your sweet face,' and he hands the warm thing – it's not a flannel because they'll chuck it away soon and I'll have another. What a waste. I've complained about the waste but it didn't get me anywhere. He rinses it and I mop up the suds that are going in my eyes. When I've used the towel he says, 'There, you're done for now. Bath tomorrow.'

'She used to shut me in the cupboard under the stairs.'

He stops folding the towel. 'Who did?'

'Aunty Bet. She was a bitch of a woman. Brenda's mother. Big woman. Used to wear a wrap around apron all day thinking she'd be clean and pristine like her house. If I made the slightest mess I'd be in that cupboard.'

'Sure that's a dreadful thing to do, Rosie. When was this?'

He comes down to my level and holds my hand. Gentle hands like Michael's. Oh, let me think of Michael not this and I regret opening my mouth.

'Don't tell the others; I won't hear the last of it and I'd rather forget it – I can forget everything else.'

'But perhaps you need to get it out into the open, now.'

'I've probably made it up. Can't remember what's real and what's not, these days. And I was a weak thing. I let her do it.'

His arm is around my shoulders and I love it but he gets up, slowly and his urgency to get me into the dining room has slowed.

'Rosie, Darlin' . . .'

'Just get me in there with the half dead and I'll slurp down whatever concoction is put in front of me.'

'Ah, here she is, says Didi. 'What you been doin' with that lady all this time, Malcolm? I can see her glasses all steamed up.'

The dining room erupts with laughter as usual as I'm handed over and she seats me next to Janet who is already shovelling in some slop so I don't get the usual happy smile. I slump in the chair and wait for my cup of tea.

'I THINK YOU might have broken these on purpose, Rosemary,' and she waves the twisted frame in front of me as I stare at my porridge. 'Did she do that, Brenda? She wants new ones, I suppose. Getting to that age. I want, I want. Bare in mind that we're not made of money. Uncle Alec is not a rich man no matter what this town might think. And this year you'll be off to the grammar school. That's a fortune in itself.'

'She stood on them by mistake, Mum. I was there. She didn't mean to.'

'Thank you, Brenda; you're a kind girl but she's got to learn to be careful. You both have. You'll stay here with me today, Rosemary. You're too clumsy.'

'But we're going to the woods with – '

'Well, *you* can go, Brenda. Rosemary stays here.'

'Awe, Mum,' Brenda wails.

I take my time forcing the porridge down. It's vile but I say nothing; it's the safest way.

I go into the cupboard under the stairs like a kitten, into the shadows, into the dark and enclose myself amongst the dirty old coats on hooks and the smelly raincoats, the dusty old shoes, the spiders and the cardboard boxes full of shoe polish, old dusters, tins of nails and screws and hammers. So different to the rest of the house. She bolts the door top and bottom. I can just about sit and I can just about stand with my head bent but have to stay there until she lets me out. It's hot in the summer and cold in winter but I never say anything. She knows she can do as she pleases, and that I won't tell. I'll stay there in the dark and melt into the shadows and shiver or sweat and listen as she messes around in the kitchen, humming along to the wireless.

'I love that song,' says Janet. 'Nat King Cole. Takes me back.'

I shake myself. 'And why would anyone in their right mind want to be, 'taken back'?'

'Well there's not much point in going forward,' says What's-His-Name, the coughing man. 'We all know where that'll end up.'

'Well, I've got a lot to be thankful for,' says Janet.

'Hubby coming in today?' he asks.

'I think so.'

'You love him?'

'Of course I do, Arthur. And I'll be going home to him as soon as he can manage me.'

There's a hush in the dining room and Nat King Cole sings the last words of *'Unforgettable'*.

It wasn't the same after Brenda's lies. Oh, how I hated her then. And mostly because I realised they might not be lies after all. But I can't get the sequence of things right. How it all seemed to escalate after her last visit that summer. Everyone seemed to know what was going on except me – or what had gone on.

I can sit here in the sitting room in a deep easy chair with floral covers and greasy patches and I can rest my head on an antimacassar and I can be deep in my thoughts when someone, the woman with the . . . Freda, perhaps might come in shuffling with her zimmer and ask for the TV, then that's the end of the peace and quiet and all my thoughts are scrambled. No wonder they think I'm a misery. Who was it who once said, You only remember the good times as a child? Well. that's a lie for a start. I might not be able to remember everything but what I do remember is pretty awful. I was terrified. There was Ma always red eyed who kept telling me that everything was all right when I knew it wasn't and Pa in a world of his own – a violent and starving world that brought anger and hate to the surface and it landed on Ma. And me. Ian Penny and Roger Aplin thought he was weird. Used to whisper when they saw me. Perhaps they hid the truth from me. But when Margaret's ma slapped my ma's face that day and it went all round the school in whispers and laughter I began to get the meaning of it. I wanted to think that Brenda had lied. But she hadn't.

SHE WAS STANDING at the water's edge. Always the water's edge. The gentle ripples covering her feet and the wet sand under her toes being dragged out to sea and she was shrieking and giggling and running around. Her swimsuit was sleek and fitted close to her body, her long legs longer than mine. She was, what? Thirteen? And always wanting to impress me with the stuff she knew but I knew she hadn't passed her eleven plus because she was at a secondary school by then.

Her hair is pinned up and she's got that smirky look that says, I know something that you don't know.

'Do you want me to tell you something very private?'

'All right.'

She dances about and it seems to me that the sun and

the bluest of blue skies are all around her and her hair glitters with it.

I'm standing on the wet sand in Brenda's hand-me-down swimsuit that is too big. Blue stretchy material that Ma calls 'rouched' as if it's better quality. I feel like a poor girl, like Veronica at school. Smelly Knickers.

I bite my fingernails.

'Don't do that, you'll end up with ugly hands.'

Then she runs off, arms all over the place like she's dancing and without telling me anything at all.

THAT'S NOT ALL of it. I want so hard to remember. Something's locked away in what grey matter I have left. I can imagine those brain cells popping like bubble wrap.

Freda stops all flow of thought when she's pushed into the sitting room waving a Union Jack and singing Land of Hope and Glory but forgetting some of the words and replacing them with, 'La La Dum Dum Di Dum'. It's the foreign nurse who's doing the pushing. She's one of the ones with an accent. European. I think she's Polish or . . .

'Hi there, Rosie. Caroline is coming in for a sing song in a minute or two or three.'

'But there's only me and Freda.'

'I am collecting others. Must make it worth the effort'

'Well, I want to leave. I'll go back to my room.'

'Oh, what is it you say? Spoil sport?' She turns the wheelchair so it's aligned with me and Freda's voice is piercing.

'I have a lot of thinking to do.'

'Still sorting out your nightmares, Rosie?'

'There's a nightmare somewhere, that's for sure. It's like a constant headache, no, like my head is whizzing all the time. Like a roulette wheel, spinning. But what is it going to stop at. I wish it would stop at something nice, maybe like Ernie.'

'What is this, Ernie?'

Michael comes in with somebody in a wheelchair. It's the cougher. 'He's a computer who dishes out money every month, Elena. If you're lucky. A bit like gambling. You buy bonds with numbers and hope they come up.'

'Michael, have I got Premium Bonds?'

'Don't know that one, Rosie, Darlin'.'

'Well, could you check with the one in navy? The nice one.'

'That's not in his remit, Rosie,' Elena says, 'You must ask her yourself.'

'Huh, you know I'll forget. But while we're at it, could you take me to see the sea one of these days?' I smile very sweetly but it takes an effort because of the smell that's like an aura around Freda.

Malcolm says, 'That might be something really good to do, Rosie. I'll give it some thought but I'll have to ask Jennifer.'

'Ah, she's the one.'

'Buckle like a dinner plate,' adds Elena with a soft laugh in Malcolm's direction.

There's a sudden flash of clarity. 'That's the other one,' I say. 'I told that to someone in confidence.'

But they're not listening; they're like a pair of conspirators now, heads together, touching hands, eye to eye. Laughing at nothing. He's a dark horse.

'I don't want to sing,' I say. 'I want to go back to my room.'

'Awe, Rosie, my lovely, sure I'll take you to the sea but Elena will come too. It'll be grand.'

I knew it. Michael and Elena. Who'd have thought?

Then he's next to me, on his haunches holding my hand and I feel a fool getting all steamed up. Just a silly old fool loving his arms in that short-sleeved tunic. Tanned and hairy. I so want to touch his arms.

'Take me back to my room, Malcolm. Please.'

He kisses my forehead and stands up straight. 'C'mon then, Rosie my love. I'll get your zimmer.'

Bloody, fucking zimmer!

THAT'S RIGHT, ROSIE, you're a fool. Always been a fool. Taking in Brenda's lies; thinking that she knows more than me. Always right. Know all. And Michael?

Meeting him was a wonder but Brenda was there as usual ready to take over from stupid me who was sitting in the shadows. Oh, yes. With bandaged hands. Oh, yes. It all comes back. Boxing Day and I'm at Michael's house in Warren Road with Brenda; scalded hands from the kettle in Aunty's kitchen, looking like a boxer; unable to wash myself let alone put any make-up on.

'You clumsy, wretched girl. All this trouble.'

And me, sitting close to the fire in the back room while

Michael and Brenda dance. Her hands all over him. And Danny and Declan and two other girls. Pretty Maureen and Plain Pat. I'm a right one saying, 'plain' when no one is as plain as me with my thin face in glasses and unwashed hair.

Michael comes over after dancing and squats down at my side and starts to poke the fire. It makes the red and orange sparks fly up the chimney and they crisp and crackle.

'So, why so silent now?' His voice is like velvet and he places chestnuts very correctly on the edge of the grate.

'What is there to talk about?'

'Why, there's the weather, the fire, the time of year, the dancers, the dreadful pictures on the wall - my mother's choice I'm sorry to say. Ah, ha, that's made you smile. You're Rosie, aren't ye? Been watchin' from afar. All tied up with those hands. Incapacitated.'

His laugh is like spring has just popped into view. He pulls off his jumper and rolls up the cuffs of his shirt sleeves. Hands, wrists and arms like a fantasy. Warm and hairy.

He whispers, *'C'mere now and dance with me. We can put our arms around each other like the others and enjoy the slowness.'*

It's like the most natural thing to do. Wrap my arms around his neck. Slide up close and smell his underarm sweat. His cheek against mine, hot and clammy but oh, so divine and his hands on my back, pulling me in.

'D'you like this, Rosie?' he says against my ear.

'Oh, I do.'

Then later, the kiss in the outhouse.

THE OTHER ONE in the navy comes in to my room with a man I haven't seen before.

'I didn't hear you knock.'

'I apologise, Rosie but your door was open. You remember Dr Pearce?'

'Never seen him before.'

He sits on the edge of my bed. Makes himself at home all right. Looks about seventeen. Not handsome. Don't like the beard.

He takes out a stethoscope from his jacket pocket and plays with it.

'Sister tells me you're breathing is deteriorating.'

'Well, Sister is wrong. My breathing is hunky dory. You know that album?'

'Beg pardon.' He looks bemused, no doubt expecting me to be demented.

'Sister?'

'David Bowie, Doctor. One of his.'

'Ah.' He gives me one of those 'humouring' smiles and pats my hand. 'Of course.'

'What do you mean, 'of course'? You couldn't have been around in the seventies.'

'No, but everyone knows Bowie.'

'Not this lot. We're all supposed to enjoy Al Bowlly and Dickie Valentine and Mantovani but what we need is

Radiohead and R.E.M. Though by the look of some of them out there they can't be bothered with music anyway. Just here to fade away.'

'Do you know what R.E.M. stands for, Rosie?'

Testing my level of dementia. I know what he's up to.

'Bugger me, Doctor. How do you expect me to remember that?'

'Can I check you over, Rosie? Must get a move on.' He sticks the end of his stethoscope under his arm to warm it. I feel like saying, my crotch would be warmer than there but I don't. He listens to my chest and back and gives Sister a look that says, I don't like the sound of that. Why not say it? They think we're all half wits. Then he checks my blood pressure with his kit and then pulls the duvet up from the bottom of the bed and looks at my legs. They are not pretty. In fact I can see for myself that they've been leaking through the stockings.

'Oh, dear. Is this new, Sister?'

'Oh, dear. Yes it is.'

Now they have to have the stockings off and they're sticking to my legs. Now they've done it. Pulled off flaky, pasty skin and there's a pong. That's it then. Gangrene and rot setting in. Old ticker giving up, at last. About time.

'Well, if I've to get ready for the Pearly Gates then I want something done about that door. There's something, someone who stands outside it most nights and threatens to come in. And I'd like it sorted. Or Saint Peter might not let me in.'

'Ah,' says the doctor.

'Yes,' says Sister.

'And can you get in touch with my cousin, Brenda, Sister. I need to sort out some very important issues before I'm dead.'

FOR SOME REASON Pa comes to mind. He was a man who seemed half alive for most of the time, apart from the rare occasions when he smiled or took me to the cove or tried to protect me from grief. After Ma died he became a ghost. His anger settled also after her death but Ma always said his anger was because of his experiences. I don't think I even bothered to try and understand what he suffered in the war but now I need to keep him in my thoughts or he'll be gone, or going like so many other things.

He's making a dip where he's sitting on the edge of my bed. 'We have to work together, Rosie but I've got to make a living and it's hard. There's no work round here and we might have to move.'

'What? From here? From the sea? From the cove?

'I need a car to get around and right now we can't afford it and there's not a market round here for fancy cabinets. I need to work for somebody. Change what I do completely.'

'But I don't want to move, Pa.'

'I can't do the complicated stuff any more, Rosie. My head is like a sieve.'

'Because of Ma?'

'Partly.' His eyes well up. Pools ready to spill over.

'And because of the Nips?'

There's a sudden beam of light from his smile and my

beating heart relaxes for a fraction of a minute.

'But try not to worry; we'll get by.'

'I don't want to leave, Pa. I love Margaret and her Ma is kind to me.'

'I know. I know. But life isn't always nice.'

'You could marry Margaret's ma. Her hubby is dead.'

Such a simple solution.

'It's not as easy as that.' His head goes down in that now familiar way and he's looking at his hands, so big in his lap. I look at his hands but remember the kittens so I look at his braces holding up his trousers and his check shirt and his brown shoes and his moustache and wonder why Ma and Pa stopped kissing such a long time ago.

BRENDA DOESN'T COME for over a fortnight by which time my legs are no better and I have to keep them up most of the time. But it's a beautiful day and I can't help smiling. I'm warm all over and the window is open letting in air that's worth breathing in so I ask the one in navy if I can go outside onto the patio.

They won't let me walk because I might exhaust myself, it's so hot. And I'll need my sun hat and must sit in the shade and must put on sun cream and have a drink of water and so it goes on until I'm plonked under the awning and can hardly feel the sun at all, not like when Brenda and I danced around on the beach avoiding the pebbles, hopping around on the red hot sand and the wet sand at the water's edge.

'Look who I've found, Rosie?' It's Didi leading Brenda plus walking stick as she finds her feet between the uneven paving slabs and the weeds.

'Didi,' I say, 'I know your name.'

'About time, Girl.' She roars with laughter as she always does but I'm thinking, it's taken a huge effort to sift through my brain to remember it.

'Rosie, Dear.' Brenda can still bend down far enough to peck my cheek. 'I've been summoned.'

'By whom?'

'By you, Rosie,'

'Where's What's-Her-Name?'

'Lorna? She's taken Finn to the play park.'

Didi brings a chair.

'Sit down, Girl.'

'I'm hardly a girl, Nurse, not with these knees.' She chuckles and winces as she sits and hands Didi the flowers she's brought.

'I'm assuming this is important, Rosie/?'

'Well, as far as I'm concerned, it is. I'm dementing, I know it. I'm struggling to remember anything these days and I need answers before I go completely ga-ga.'

'You seem bright as a button to me.'

'Well, that's how it goes sometimes. Now. How come you've got your wits and I haven't? I was the one who went to grammar school. I was the one who went to college.'

'It doesn't work like that.'

'Hmm. So tell me why you're here.'

'I'm here because you want to talk about something

important, I think.'

Her grey hair is still tinged with gold and is soft, fine and wavy.

'You've kept your good looks, Brenda,' I sniff. 'Always managed to get the boys.'

'Let's not go there, Rosie; it will cause unnecessary grief.'

'I still grieve, Brenda. Nothing goes away. I grieve in the day and in the night. And it all comes down to you. The hurting. The fear. No, the fear was the haunting. It was the hurting with you and your bitch of a mother, Aunty Bet. She knew what she was doing and so did you.'

'If you're going to be nasty, Rosie then I shall go. I'll ring Lorna to collect me.'

'What was all that about at the cove? Why spread all that, whatever it was. You knew it would hurt me. We'd had such good times together. And Ma was always good to you.'

'I really don't know what you're going on about.'

'Oh, yes you do, you spineless woman.'

That shuts her up. She sits there pursing her lips and looking around in case anyone has heard.

I let her stew for a minute.

It was a hot day just like today. The tide was in and the waves were rippling over our feet, cooling us, bringing in the weed, rubbery and brown, tubes and ribbons and it would stay there when the tide went out ready for the gulls to pick over. And you said . . .

Oh, here it comes. 'Your dad isn't really your dad is he?'

I didn't understand what she was saying. 'Course he is.'

'I heard Mum talking to Aunty Vi and my mum's not a liar.'

'You're a liar then.'

She looks at me for a long time. 'You didn't know, did you?'

I start to hate Brenda. 'Pa was a prisoner,' I say. 'I know *that*. *You* don't know that.'

'Oh, but I do. Everybody knows. '

My skin is burning, I can tell and my hair is sticking to my forehead wet, like the seaweed.

She continues her cruelty. 'Your Ma loved another man. You are his *love-child.*'

She says the words like she's known forever and that she knows she shouldn't be saying them and like she's smirking without smiling and I think she knows that I don't really understand.

'Your Mum loved another man,' she confirms, 'but your dad doesn't know. Or maybe he does. It's very romantic, though, don't you think?'

Then she looks as if she might be sorry for what she's said because she looks at the ground and she pokes around with her hair and says, 'Let's swim,' and she runs into the cool sea.

Ooohhhhhhh!

PART TWO

They've banned the salt.

I've put in a complaint to the ones in navy but they have an answer for everything. They come back with waterwork trouble or high blood pressure or swollen ankles or . . .

'But you can't have a tomato sandwich without salt,' I argue.

'Or a boiled egg,' says Arthur.

'Or pepper. Black pepper, white pepper.' says Freda.

'We're not talking about condiments per se, Freda. It's the absence of salt that we're on about.'

Janet pipes up with, 'We'll all get used to it in time.'

'That's always been the thing with old people,' I mutter. 'We take it all and don't complain. We don't matter. Who, on this table really knows what medication we're on?'

Typically no one says anything or can't be bothered.

'And what's the point of banning it at this late stage of our lives?'

'Is that you stirrin' it all up again, Rosie?' It's Didi. 'Thought you'd given up. Thought you'd mellowed.'

'She'll never mellow, that one,' says Arthur. 'Acid thoughts. Acid tongue.

'Rosie.' It's a different voice, soft and close to my ear. The nice one in navy.

'I'm asleep. And I'm too hot.'

'I need to look at your legs. See how they're doing.'

'They're doing nothing; just hanging there on the end of my torso.'

There are chuckles all round and I realise that I might have said something funny, but whatever it was it's disappeared into the air and I'm forced upright by someone and my hands are clamped onto the Zimmer.

'Am I going to bed?'

'Not now, Rosie. I want to look at your legs. We're going to the treatment room.'

'That pansy of a doctor coming?'

'I don't know who you mean.'

'That pansy. That starling in the shiny suit.'

She stops outside a door.

'Doors are the bane of my life.'

She manoeuvres me through into the room and starts putting dressings on a trolley with bandages and tape on the shelf below. Then she fetches a foot stool, covers it with a paper sheet and begins unravelling the stockings until she's down to the dressings underneath.

'It's a bit smelly this week, Rosie. Might be brewing something. Ah, Elena,' she says when the door is opened, 'just in time. Take off the dressing while I wash my hands, will you?'

'Have I got gangrene?'

'Don't be silly, Rosie. It will heal,' says Elena.

They're both standing at the sink now, scrubbing and muttering. Anyone would think that I'm going under the knife. They're pulling on their rubber gloves. I'm contaminated, that's what it is; contaminated with guilt and bad thoughts.

'I want to ask something.'

'What?' they both question.

'Malcolm and this one want to take me to see the sea.'

'Oh, that's new to me,' says the Nice One. 'What do you know about it, Elena?'

'I think we were talking about it some days ago.'

'You lived near the sea as a child, I believe?'

She's doing something to the ulcer. Poking it.

'Ow!'

'Just taking a swab.'

'They were mostly happy days until Brenda stirred things up.'

'Your cousin?'

'It's always been a conundrum to me how my grandmother spawned three girls so different. My mother, the youngest was a saint until I was conceived by all accounts. Her sisters Betty and Vi were devils. Both must be dead now, thank God. Both spread lies about Ma and Pa when we lived by the sea.'

'Would you like to go back there for a visit?'

Now there's a thought to drift with . . .

The sun would go down behind the offshore reef like a slow sinking fire. Glowing oranges and reds and streaky yellows, changing shape all the time; thin clouds moving slowly and Ma swimming in the cove would make hardly a ripple on the sparkling water. She was a mermaid and a water baby rolled into one, drifting on her back, sculling with her hands. All this amid the smell of dead fish and seaweed and the sound of flies, bluebottles, bees and wasps crawling into empty Corona bottles and crisp packets flapping and dancing . . . Beauty and ugliness living side by side.

'Rosie?'

'I'd need to think about it.'

'Well, it's possible. If we can fund it.'

'Have I got money?'

'You still have savings.'

'And my pension?'

'It's included in your savings.'

'But who pays for me here?' I'm so hot I think I might faint even though I'm in the chair. It's like a hot flush. That's the trouble, no air. And the door is closed. 'Can someone open the door? I'm suffocating.'

She's pulling up a stocking. 'We're nearly done. We'll try without bandages for a while longer, Rosie. This is more comfortable.' She straightens up, her knuckles in the small of her back. 'And you're asking who pays. Brenda is your next of kin and has power of attorney. But I think all the details will be with your solicitor.'

'I've got a solicitor?' I can hardly believe it.

'Of course.'

'And do I have a will?' This is all new to me and a lot to take in.

'I'll get her to come and see you.'

'Who?' I'm getting breathless now.

'Hopefully your cousin and your solicitor.'

'Would they know what happened to Margaret? My best friend at school.'

'They will be the ones to ask.'

THE GRIEF AFTER Ma's death was tempered a little by living with Margaret and her Ma. Pa decided he couldn't look after me anymore. I was lonely in the cottage in spite of me being with him but it wasn't just his silent weirdness, he was a man of few words anyway. He did less and less in his workshop and walked more and more along the pebbled beach in his brown boots and shabby jacket. Whatever the weather he would disappear and I would be left to clear the dishes or poke the fire. But he scared me – not as much as the thing outside my bedroom door but more like filling me with worry. Deep worry. Overwhelming anxiety; that's a better word.

Sometimes I would follow him in my wellies and mac and I would trudge some way behind him and it would be better than staying in the cottage on my own. . . .

His jacket is flying open in the wind and because the wind is coming my way I can hear it flapping along with his trousers around his lower legs and I listen to the crunch,

crunch, crunch of his boots. He's hunched, his shoulders bent forward, his neck disappearing into his collar. Then his hands are in his wet hair smoothing it back and then in his pockets, deep and dry. And I am trailing behind and dusk is coming in and the clouds are thick with rain, grey and scary because I know how much it will pour any second and we're stuck out here on the beach going nowhere and me in red wellies that are pinching.

Suddenly he turns and we both stop walking. He can just about see me in my mac that's a hand-me-down from Brenda. It must look black in the dark. He stands there looking at me and scratches his head.

'Rosie?' he calls and I can hear it very faint as it drifts with the wind past my ear.

'Pa?'

I don't think he can hear me because I only mutter, afraid to speak too loudly. Yet I want him to hear. I want him to see I'm here. It's like he's sleeping, like he's in a dream and he might shout if he wakes suddenly. But he plods towards me and I can see that he's trying to smile because his face becomes softer and eventually he's beside me, his arm around my shoulder, heavy but comforting and he says, 'This has got to stop.'

I wonder if it's the walking up and down on the beach that has to stop or me following him but we are soon home in front of the fire that's still going because I put on more logs and he's bringing in a biscuit and a cup of warm milk . . .

They don't know that half of every night is spent with my eyes on the door, recalling or trying to recall aspects of my life. They say I snore or cough or mumble in my sleep. I know that every night there's something that creeps out of my head and it's not just me going dotty, it's me remembering and deep down I remember a lot, it's just that it's jumbled and I can't stop the bad things and struggle to recall the nice things. Were there nice things? I know there was. Somewhere.

As I lie in my bed under the soft duvet I try to stop thinking about the stockings gripping my legs and the rasping of my breath and put my hands on my skinny old breasts and wonder if I can bring my nipples out. Have to be careful because you're never really alone here and anyone could suddenly barge in and find me touching them. I have to pull up my nighty to get to them and sure enough they have disappeared. Makes me flush, though. Oh. . .

. . . What do you think you're doing, Rosemary?

I tug at my nightie, my heart beating like a hammer.

'Are you playing with yourself? You dirty girl!'

'No, Aunty. I had an itch.'

'You're a mucky girl. Don't you dare let me catch you doing that again; it'll get into a filthy habit. You'll be going off the rails like your mother.'

And she's out of my room like a . . . like a . . .

Oh, Ma . . .

... That came from the depths. A memory I'd rather forget. She was a horror, Aunty Bet. Dead in her grave now.

The bitch.

Sweaty Betty on the jetty, full of sin, push her in, get her wetty. How I used to laugh to myself when I made that up. I could bring it up in my thoughts whenever I was locked in the cupboard or slapped or . . .

'Aunty, open the door. Let me out. I'm suffocating.'
'Say, "Please."'

I TRY AND think of Michael. He could get my nipples out. Did he know instinctively how to do it? How to do all those things? Did it come naturally to him?

. . . My hand is in the shallow of his back and I run my fingers up to his broad shoulders and up to the back of his neck. His mouth is next to my ear. His breath warm, his voice a whisper.

'You'll be a feckin' good fuck, Rosie when I can get inta ye. You'll be on fire.'

'WE'RE GETTING A group together, Rosie to go to the seaside tomorrow. We've got a driver and we can take four of you at a time. We can do a couple trips over the summer. We're thinking, you and Janet, Freda and Arthur. In truth, My Dear, there's not many who want to go.'

It's that new one with her badges and buckle. Tight hair and tight lips. Standing in my doorway.

'Sounds good,' I say. 'Thank you.' I'd better be subservient or they won't let me go.

'I'm afraid we can't get to your seaside home town, it's too far; we'll have to go somewhere closer.'

'I don't want to go there anyway. There are bad memories.'

'Well, try not to think about them, Dear.'

I try that all the time, doesn't she know that? But thoughts are always there, rummaging around. I imagine trying to get wheelchairs onto those pebbles or trying to walk with a Zimmer and us gasping because there's nowhere to get a cup of tea or an ice cream. Or maybe there is now; or worse than that, nowhere to have a pee.

That was a long time ago so things might have improved, gone upmarket. But I guess the place is still smelly and miserable.

'The place was smelly and miserable.'

'But it must have been lovely in the summer?'

She's got no imagination.

'It went downhill after Ma died.'

'Oh. Well, no doubt it did.'

She flounces off.

Elena flounces in.

'Are you escorting us to the seaside?'

She puts the Zimmer within reach. 'Don't know yet, Rosie.' I struggle to the edge of the bed and she hoiks me up. 'Would you rather have the chair this morning?'

She means am I likely to wee before I get to the lav in which case she'll get the Holy Chair with a pan in it.

'No, today I'll be fine.'

I'm on the lav and having trouble getting started. Elena turns on the tap and lets the water run full pelt into the wash basin . . .

. . . as I'm made to sit on the toilet bowl. Aunty slaps my face. Not hard, she doesn't want Uncle Alec to hear. 'You pee in the toilet, Rosemary, not in the bed.' She's whispering, her face down close to mine, her breath smelling of gravy from the meat pie. 'How many times . . ? You're too old for this to happen. I've got Brenda leaving school next year and you've regressed. I'm the one having to deal with this sort of malarkey. You're not a baby any more . . .'

I pee and Elena turns off the tap. 'Good girl,' she says. Huh!

MALCOLM PUTS A cup of tea on the breakfast table.

The sun is pouring through the main windows and it touches our faces. They'll be in their wheelchairs, pushing their zimmers and attempting to race with their sticks to get out, but it'll only be to the weedy patio and there will be a spill, a trip or a fall on those uneven slabs, for sure.

'I want to go home,' says Freda. She staggers over holding on to the chair backs and tugs at Malcolm's sleeve.

'D'ye want me to open those windows, ladies? Or pull the curtain over or whatever?'

Janet says, 'I don't mind. The sunshine is lovely.'

'It's like an oven in here.' I mutter, 'I can hardly breathe.'

I watch Freda sigh as she waits for him to reach up and pull the sash down, then he moves to another window but there's hardly any air to come in because there's too much heat rushing out. When he reaches up this time I catch a glimpse of the top of his trousers which are hanging on his slim hips and there's a flash of flesh. Ha! No T-shirt today. I glance at Janet but she's still munching her toast. Crumbs all over the table and down her front. It's no good sharing the excitement with her; she's not interested; she's got Hubby. If he had the chance he'd get her home and get her into bed. That's the sort of man he is, I suspect. He's smarmy.

'Now, Rosie. Tell me why the straight face this mornin'?'

'It's always straight,' coughs Arthur.

Malcolm is down at my level and I can see down the V of his tunic. 'C'mon, me darlin', I thought we were friends. Thought you liked me. Why the scowl, now? '

His hand is over mine and there are a few soft hairs on his fingers. His nails are finely clipped and clean. Freda is stepping from one foot to the other, hovering.

'Are you taking us to see the sea?' I whisper.

'Yep, I think so.'

He raises himself and towers over me.

'Is Elena coming with us?'

'Yep, I hope so. Right, Freda, let's get you back to your chair now.'

I'M IN THE shadows again but on the patio and the sun is casting its glorious light between the moving leaves and branches of the huge beach tree. The light filters onto the ground and flickers on Freda's frowning face as she shakes the table that's keeping her trapped in the high-backed chair.

'I want to go home.'

It's just too depressing.

'Shut up, Freda, there's a good girl.' Oh, God Almighty, I'm turning into them. 'Freda, we're going to the seaside tomorrow. Think about it.'

And I try and think about it but it doesn't come. Instead I'm in the woods not wanting to go home. Not wanting to go back to where Aunty Bet is watching my every move. I let my thoughts go wild and take it as it comes. And there's Michael with his hair the way it was, and Declan and red headed Danny and there's Brenda and me and Pale Faced Pat in the green and shady woods, walking the paths, stepping over roots, slipping on wet leaves. Brenda is flirting around the boys as usual and Pale Face is trying to keep up with her. Then Brenda and Declan start to wrap their arms around each other and Michael stares at them until eventually he waits for me to catch up. Pat is left with Danny and I can tell that she's not interested in him. She keeps pushing him away, but he still sniffs round her like a dog even so and I have to be careful or Brenda might tell Aunty so I beg Michael to stay at arms length. He keeps his hands in his pockets and his head down watching his feet.

'So many feckin' rules, Rosie.'

'I can't help it, Michael, I can't.'

'Jesus, Rosie, I want to kiss you.'

'I want you to. I really do.'

'Meet me later, then and we can . . . y'know.'

I know only too well. 'But Brenda will want to come. That, or the Bitch will stop me.'

'When can you get out of that feckin' house for good?

'She won't be able to control me when I go to college. And I don't want to make a fuss in case she forces me to quit. She'll probably say that she wants another wage coming in. Even though Brenda's qualified now she doesn't earn much at the salon. But she still gushes and flirts and I'm . . .'

'Still a wee girl as lovely as a primrose. And what's with the 'salon'?

'They call it a salon. So bloody high-falutin' when all you want is a shampoo and set.' I mimic his accent and he laughs and puts his arm around my shoulder.

He draws me closer. *'But they're not wantin' for money, are they?'*

I'm so comfortable strolling in the woods with him as he holds my hand and the pigeons call to each other and the blackbirds sing into the sun.

'You're a wee wren hidin' in the bushes timid and quiet, happy listenin' to the breeze and the rustlin' leaves.'

'No, Ma was the, "wee wren", not me. She was so dainty.'

We turn to each other and his arms are around me and I feel his heart under his jumper thumping away like a bird in my hand.

'You'll come back at the end of term, won't ye?'

'You know I will. And will you wait for me?'

'Aye, I'll be here. Give me that kiss now, Brenda is well ahead.'

So we kiss and his lips are divine and his tenderness

overwhelms me. He takes off my glasses, pockets them and holds my face in his hands.

'Darlin' Rosie,' he says. *'I do love you.'*

AFTER WE'VE SWELTERED in the heat on the patio they take us in one by one to use the lav. It's potty training. I'm not daft, I can see the point but it doesn't always work with the other. I can't regulate my insides to cooperate with laxatives and when you call for someone and it's urgent it can be embarrassing. That's another fear. Losing it completely and having no control. All of us here are ruled by our bladders and bowels. We have reverted to children needing adults to look after us. The circle of life and death. I know I'm on my way bit by bit and can do nothing about it but I don't want the dreams any more. Or the fears. I can see that Freda is permanently in agony with hers. Fingers scratching, hands wringing, knuckles whitening. Then I realise I'm doing the same.

IT WAS ABOUT the time when Brenda started telling her lies that weren't lies after all that Pa would stomp about in the parlour not wanting to go to the workshop and he would eventually flop out in the armchair by the fire as if the world was against him. And Ma would stand there – I can see her in her green paisley dress and flowery pinny leaning, fists on the sink, her head bent down so far that I couldn't see if she was sad or angry but whatever it was made my stomach turn over.

Pa starts to snore and it's only three o'clock and there's a hammering on the back door. I'm in the shadows at the bottom of the stairs where the old coats are; a space behind the smelly curtain that's rarely pulled fully across, so I can see what's going on. Ma straightens up and Pa wakes up, startled. He makes no attempt to stand so it's Ma who opens the door. She takes a deep breath first and then she lifts the latch and there is Gracie, Margaret's Ma standing in the doorway breathing heavy and I can see there's going to be trouble. I feel afraid and want Pa to get up and join them to calm the air.

Slap! Right across Ma's face, so hard that she's knocked off balance and her hand is up to her cheek and she staggers to hold on to the sink and Gracie starts to cry enormous sobs.

'You slut! You bloody slut!'

'Gracie . . .' Ma's soft voice.

'You couldn't even keep your mouth shut about it, could you? Telling Betty. Telling Vi. All of you wondering who she'd look like.'

'You don't understand, Gracie. Please.'

'And we've been such friends. What a fool I've been all this time.'

She's gasping in air and standing in the same spot, heaving. Then she turns and runs off, her bare legs white and her hair blowing around.

Ma turns and sees me on the bottom step biting my nails and Pa is at my side and we both look at her as she touches her red cheek again . . .

It's red hot in the people carrier so Malcolm opens the windows first and then helps us in. Elena is at his beck and call and I decide to watch them closely for any signs of a secret romance brewing or if it has already brewed. But she is not the right one for him; she's kind but sly and at some point I'm going to have to point it out to him because he could be easily led. So many young men, no, older men too can be discombobulated by sly women.

They are in the front seat and they've put me across the isle with Janet. What's-His-Name is blocking in Freda. She thinks this is her lucky day, she thinks that she's really going home.

It's like a school trip when I can't wait to eat my sandwiches. Tomato on white bread and they're soggy already in the brown paper bag.

Elena has got her leg up against Malcolm's but he's being very professional, not even a soft smile her way. Michael couldn't resist a smirky smile when he called at Aunty Bet's the day after the Boxing Day party . . .

'Morning, Missus. Can I see Rosie? If that's all right?'

'And you are?'

'Michael, Mrs. Byrne. From down Warren's Way. '

'And what would you want with Rosemary?'

'I met her yesterday and would like to see her again. If that's okay with you, like?'

I can see him from the bedroom window and he's smirking, thinking he's looking handsome in front of the witch. And of course he is handsome but little does he know how sharp and cutting she can be. Brenda, who can do no wrong is tripping down the stairs and at the door.

'Hi, Michael. Do you want to see me?' She edges her mother to the side. If I did that I'd get a wallop.

'Well, hello, Brenda. You're looking lovely today but it's Rosie I'm wantin' to see.' He's standing his ground and I'm upstairs smiling for once in my life.

'Rosemary!' Aunty Bet calls up the stairs. 'There's a young man here to see you.'

So I rush down, grab my coat from the hook and squeeze past Brenda with a smirk that equals Michael's.

THERE'S THE SEA, the blue and the blue-grey and the blue-green rippling all together onto the sandy beach in never ending waves. The beach is full of bronzed people, wind breaks and damp dogs. There's Malcolm unloading and there's Elena helping us to get off the carrier one by one and into the wheelchairs. Then we're plonked on the edge of the promenade looking out to the horizon and the swooping seagulls with their sunny under wings. Janet is beaming but it sounds like What's-His-Name, Arthur has been on the Woodbines again and Freda is looking bemused. This is not her home. Neither is it anything like my cove. This is a happy place and there are children with cornets and red cheeks and dads manoeuvring pushchairs and men with builder's bums and big breasted mothers with no bras under their mucky T-shirts.

Then there's the trip to the toilets, the one constant thing in my life these days, and the blankets on knees and an ice cream for each of us and I'm looking at the children hopping and skipping and screaming and swimming like water babies. What a lovely day. My first school. How I loved the children . . .

The classroom ceiling is very high, the windows arched and church like and the boy, Stephen raises his hand and waves it about in urgency.

'Miss. Miss. Why doesn't Tom drown?'

'Try not to interrupt, Stephen when I'm reading a story.'

'But, Miss . . .'

I close the book with the bookmark inside. 'Hands up those who would like to know the answer to Stephen's question?'

A sprinkling of arms is raised.

'But he does drown, Miss and it's magic that he stays alive under water.'

One bright spark in a class of thirty.

'You're right, John. You've been listening. And if you all continue to listen you eventually discover that he lives under water and grows up to be a good man and is allowed to return to human form on land. It's a fairy tale and so magical that good things happen . . .'

GOOD THINGS. A dog barks and I'm back with the oldies. Freda is transfixed by the sea. I'm not surprised. It draws you in. The waves come for you from miles away in their constant travelling and they suck at you if you're on the edge so you can't help but go with it, one foot after the other until your balance is gone and you're swept away to where it's deep and thick and it's saying, I've got you now so no more worries . . .

I am transfixed too. Today, the sun is at its brightest and the sea has become bright blue with pure white edges on the incoming gentle waves. But tomorrow it could be mixed with all colours and its claws might be out.

'And how are you enjoyin' your day, Rosie,' asks Malcolm in his soft sing song voice.

'What?' I'm shaken into reality, or what I think is reality. I don't really know any more.

'We're gettin' fish and chips any minute now,' he says. 'Just small portions 'cause you'll have supper later when we get home.'

'Am I going home?' says Freda who is suddenly alive.

Malcolm puts his hands on her shoulders as he stands behind her and pats them like Pa did to me after Ma died and he'd decided to send me off to live with Margaret and her mother . . .

'Just until I can work things out, Rosie. It won't be for long.'

'Until I can come back here?'

'Probably.'

His hands are shaking as they hover over my shoulders and I think he's lying but I love Margaret and she'll be excited but I'm not sure about her ma after the slapping last year and wonder what she feels about it now . . .

'Malcolm.' I call him over and ask him to bend down to my level and whisper over the sound of the sea and the shouting children. 'Put your hands on my shoulders like you did there with Freda. Will you?'

And without saying anything he does it and keeps them there while my thoughts go back to Pa . . .

'Why did Margaret's mother slap Ma that day?' I ask him.

'She was angry with her.'

'I know that. But why was she so angry? She wasn't angry with you. Tell me, Pa.'

'I will one day.'

But I know. Brenda knew and I thought she'd lied. Aunty Bet and Aunty Vi knew. I've been left in the dark but I remember what Brenda said that day on the beach.

'You're not really my pa, are you?' I ask it so quietly it's as if I don't want him to hear me so he can't answer but I know it's true.

And he doesn't answer he just replaces his hands on my shoulders so I can't see his face . . .

I put my right hand onto Malcolm's left hand and hold his fingers.

Why is it that whenever I can gather together some calm and just a miniscule amount of joy I drift off and encounter demons? It really stirs my stomach and it does today, by the sea, in the sun, warm and cosy and I think I might throw up all the fish I enjoyed so much. The seagulls are having fun squabbling for bits on the ground. But there's something well back in my head that springs to mind and I don't like it so I push it back and try to stop thinking and before we know it we're off to the toilets one by one and then packed into the people carrier.

They welcome us back like we've been away for weeks and we have to keep recalling everything and telling them about our glorious day which really only amounted to a few hours and I've forgotten most of it already. Janet gushes with information and she'll have to repeat it all when Hubby comes in.

But he doesn't come in. She beams at all the carers and the nurses and the residents but I can see that she's putting it on because her good hand is shaking and her head is nodding like it's unstable on her shoulders.

'You could ring him,' I say

'I can't use those phones. My brain is addled.'

'Ask Didi or Malcolm.'

'I'm afraid to, Rosie. He's not been feeling so well lately. And he has to get someone to drive him now.'

'Give him time, then.'

She tries to smile but then calls out; she wants to go to her room and they take her without a fuss. Then they come for me and we both disappear from the sitting room and I'm relieved for the peace and quiet but then, suddenly I'm exhausted and want to lie down but it's easier to breathe sitting up so I have to stay in my chair by the window with my feet up and I look out at the squawking jackdaws and my head falls back.

I F M A HADN'T been a wren then she would have been a bluebird and I'd say that Pa was a sparrow. Oh, I was cruel to her. Not understanding anything at that age and angry that Brenda was always right and Pa so mild and accepting. Most of the time. But I didn't know the half of it or if I did I've forgotten.

'Tell me about my real Pa,' I scowl at Ma as she takes a casserole or a pie or whatever it is out of the oven. She throws the tea towel towards the sink but it falls to the floor and such a little thing and she's in tears again.

'Tell me about my real Pa.' I shout this time in spite of knowing that she heard me the first time. 'Brenda was right. She told me stuff last year.'

Ma's chest is going in and out and I can hear her breathing. I start to feel sick. 'Why did Margaret's ma slap you? How can that be right? '

'You know nothing, Rosie but I'll tell you one day. All you need to know is that I loved your real Pa.'

'And you don't love my wrong Pa?'

'I thought I did, once.'

Then he comes through the back door and takes off his cap. He looks at me and then at Ma, hangs it on the peg and lets out a deep sigh as if he's heard what Ma just said.

'Get to your room, Rosie.' He says it with that awful harshness again and I decide it's time for me to shut up and do as he says because he has big hands and they frighten me...

I'M RELIEVED TO wake from my half sleep when What's-Her-Name, Lottie, comes in with a chair and there's Brenda hobbling with her stick.

Ha, the raven, and behind her is a thin streak of lightening. A stork.

'You summoned us, Rosie,' says the Raven as she sits down. She looks around for somewhere to prop her stick. 'And I've brought Mrs Brownlow of Childs, Browne and Brownlow as requested.'

'Beverley, please,' the stork responds as she reaches out to shake my hand.

What's-Her-Name says 'I'll fetch another chair, Sweetie,' and she pops out.

'I didn't summon anyone.'

'Don't mess me about, Rosemary. It's not easy to get about these days. You wanted to talk about finances. Beverley is your solicitor.'

It takes a while for it to sink in and I don't know what to say.

Thingy comes in with a chair and Beverley sits down. She says,' Perhaps you'd like to talk about your will, Miss Cooper?'

'I can't remember writing a will and I don't have any money.'

'Yes, you do, My Dear.'

'And who do I leave my goods and shackles to anyway?

I don't know who is dead and who's alive.'

'Well, Brenda here is your next of kin and will be acting as executor. And she also has full power of attorney regarding finances and health issues so you have nothing to worry about.'

'You've lost me,' I close my eyes. 'Hang on a minute.' I'm suddenly energised. 'How did I get in this place? Am I sectioned? I'm not mad. Do I have money for it? Do I have money for my funeral? And who gave you permission to be all these things, Brenda?'

It's Lottie with coffee and biscuits and my brain turns muddy.

'Thank you, Nurse.' says Brenda. 'Well, you did, Rosemary. You signed everything. We decided that you were losing capacity and needed an advocate. Better to be prepared. It produces such difficulties if there's no POA arranged.

'Pa was a POA in the war,' I add to all the nonsense.

'He was a POW, Rosie. A prisoner of war.'

'I know what a POW is.' I close my eyes again.

'Miss Cooper, Rosemary, do you want to check your will?'

'Of course I want to check my will.'

I'm exhausted and I want Malcolm to send them away. I can't even remember writing a will but I say, 'All right, but if I've got to sign anything I want Malcolm here.'

Beverley rummages in her briefcase and brings out the business.

'It says here that you want all of your estate to go to

Margaret Hyde (that was) of . . .'

'She's my sister. She's my next of kin.'

'She was your half sister, Rosie,' says Brenda.

I note the 'was'.

'She's dead, Rosie. Died last year.'

Oh. I can hardly breathe.

'And in the event of her death your estate goes to Brenda here.'

Ohhh.

It's time I went on. I'm overwhelmed with bad news, bad feelings and bad memories.

This morning I woke and felt the overload of a bad dream and I thought, Another bloody day.

I say, when Malcolm comes in, 'They're taking over what's left of my existence, Michael. All my life I've been taken over by this one or that one.'

He says, sitting in the chair by my bed, 'Rosie,' and he takes my cold hand and kisses the back of it. 'We have sad news, now.'

'Then I don't want to hear it,' and I attempt to turn away from him

'Rosie, it's Janet's husband. He died yesterday afternoon.'

I roll back. 'What? Hubby?'

'Yes. He had the heart attack. Janet is very upset.'

'Of course she is. Oh, dear.'

'But, we have to carry on. Let's get you up and about and sittin' next to her lovely self and you can talk to her over breakfast.' He squeezes my hand a little and gets up so tall and handsome by my bedside.

'Who is her next of kin?' I ask.

'Her son. I'm thinking his name might be Brian.'

'She won't be going anywhere now, then? Home, I mean.'

He manoeuvres me to the edge of the bed and feeds my arms into my dressing gown. 'Sure, he would never have been able to look after her, Rosie. It was her wishful thinking.'

'There's no hope for me, then?' I give a small chuckle and try not to be too wistful and think, that's all we've got left now, then, wishful thinking.

I'm on the lav again and Ola comes in to give a hand. Her face is as long as a fiddle but I guess it's going to be like that for a few days.

'He was a good looker,' I say struggling to stand straight.

'Who?' they both ask, 'Hubby?'

'No, silly, Clint,' and I give a nod to my poster. He's grinding on that cigar. A perfect snarl, and I decide to try and drift back to Michael later when I'm alone. But that's painful even. I could do with him now, though with his arms around me. 'Michael,' I say, 'hold me close.'

'Rosie, that's not in my job description.'

Thankfully, he smiles and I say, 'Wishful thinking out loud, Malcolm.'

But Janet isn't at the breakfast table, there's a new woman with no front teeth. She's sucking her top lip in.

'Didi?' I call.

'Lovely ladies.' She arrives from nowhere. 'I'll introduce you both. Rosie this is Pauline and Pauline this is Rosie.'

'But where's Janet?'

'She wantin' her breakfast in her room this mornin'. She grievin' bad.'

I don't feel like sitting with this new one, my stomach is turning over and I feel sick and confused and she's gabbling on wanting an audience. I don't have to talk to her. It's my right to remain silent so I let her get on with it and she does. Family and children, grandchildren, names and ages of all of them and she's got one of those mobile phones with photos that go on forever. What's-His-Name appears and takes over the conversation. He saves my sanity.

Didi comes over with cornflakes and banana then bustles off for teapots and toast. But I'm not hungry, there's a pain somewhere in my body and in my head so I just poke the cornflakes around.

I POKE THE cornflakes around. Brenda has already left for work.

'Eat up, Rosemary, you'll be late.' Aunty is bustling around wanting to clear the table already. 'You'll be hungry later on, mid morning and fainting again and I'll have to walk up to that school and feel embarrassed.

'But I don't feel well, Aunty. My insides hurt.'

'Well, you're not skipping school. If we're paying out all this money for uniform and extras you'd better make it worth our while.'

So I force it down and struggle to get up from the table but my legs are wobbly and I hold on to the edge of the table. I can see it happening before it happens. I feel so small and fragile as I drop to the floor pulling the tablecloth with me and the bowl and the milk and the cornflakes and the orange squash all fall onto me and onto Aunty's precious carpet.

When the blackness disappears I vomit.

I think, I'll be in the cupboard again but Aunty doesn't say a word. She just sighs as she brings a bowl and a flannel and cleans my face. She gathers all the broken bits together in the tablecloth and takes it to the kitchen then comes back and helps me to my feet and walks me to the sofa in the sitting room.

'You rest there and then we'll get that uniform off.'

There are no raised voices, no threats or anger.

That act of kindness. One act of kindness when there's been no kindness . . .

'Where's Janet? I ask to anyone who's passing.

'In her room, Girl, having peace and quiet.' Didi gives a nod in the direction of Arthur and the new one who are huddled together.

'Can I see her?'

'I will ask as soon as I can, Rosie.'

But soon as I can is not soon enough because she is rushed into hospital with a stroke. I don't think I'll see her again.

A MAN IS standing in my doorway talking to a woman. His arm is raised and he's holding onto the door frame. She is too close. It's Michael and Brenda.

'Michael!' The loudness of my voice alarms me. 'Michael.'

'Put on your glasses now, Rosie.'

I fumble on my bedside table and find them.

He comes over to me and Elena watches from the doorway, smiling.

I whisper, 'She's making googly eyes at you. She's trying to win you over. I've seen it before. She's a prick teaser.'

Both of them erupt into guffaws and I don't know why. It wasn't a joke.

'I love you, Rosie,' he says, laughing

'I love you too, Michael. And you can leave him alone, Brenda. It's me he loves.'

. . . *'Take off your glasses now, Rosie, I want to kiss your eyes then your nose then your mouth, in that order.'*

Malcolm touches the shallow of Elena's back as he leads her out.

I WAS SUCH a weakling. A small weak thing hiding under that slippery eiderdown, listening to the raised voices downstairs. What if I'd gone down there and asked them to stop? Please, you're frightening me. Please, I can't sleep. But would they have heard my small voice behind all the racket? And I wanted Pretty to come upstairs with me but Pa wouldn't allow it but I could have slipped past them and found her and taken her with me because they wouldn't have noticed. I may as well have been invisible. Or in the shadows. Or I could have taken the wooden chiming clock off the mantelpiece, held it above my head and smashed it down onto the cold, hard lino and all the cogs and coils would have spilled out. But I didn't.

And after Ma died I could have stood my ground with Pa and refused to go to Margaret's but the fact was that I wanted to go because I felt so alone in the cottage with Pa at work long hours or not at work at all or walking the beach every night or at the Dog and Duck and then I stayed under the eiderdown and hid, or waited for him to come to bed and pretended to be asleep.

Then, at Margaret's . . .

. . . Gracie gives Margaret a huge hug. Then she gives me a hug that's not so huge but I don't think she realises and I can't expect her to. Pa drops my things in the hallway and takes off his cap. He holds it with both hands and is thanking her for taking me in.

'She'll be all right with me, Frank. And we're in the same village. You can pop in any time. It's not as if . . .' She leaves it hanging. 'Take Rosie to your room, Margie.'

But I want to hear the rest of the conversation. I know there's more to come so I stand with my foot on the first step of the stairs and look up and Margaret is at the top eager to welcome me into her house. I'm excited but know that this feeling can't last. Nothing lasts. I reach the top of the stairs, holding on to the banister while Margaret reaches our room and opens the door and I hear Gracie say, 'I'm sorry, Frank, about not taking the . . .'

'Don't worry,' says Pa. His voice is so quiet when he's not bellowing. 'I'll look after it.'

And I know what he's talking about and I want to scream at Gracie and Pa that it's Pretty they're talking about not any old cat and I'm afraid that he'll get the shovel out as soon as he gets home.

But I say nothing.

Then Margaret is pulling at my hand to follow her and we're sitting on our beds looking at each other and eventually we are laughing.

How weak is that?

AT THE BREAKFAST table I ask Didi, 'Where's Janet?'

'She in hospital, Darlin', not so good. But you got Pauline now to talk to.'

I look across the table and Pauline is chewing the cud, waiting to talk.

I try to use different tactics. 'I want Janet.'

'I don't think Janet will be coming back, Rosie.'

'Where is she, then?'

'She's just told you, you silly moo.' It's What's-His-Name again, coughing in my direction.

I feel bereft. If it wasn't for Malcolm and the nice one in navy I'd feel like cutting my throat. Everyone I've ever cared about has gone. If I start a conversation with That One she'll never stop and it'll all be rubbish. Could never abide small talk.

I try another tactic aimed at improving the conversation.

'What work did you do, Pauline?'

'When?'

'When you left school?'

'I got married. Dickie was older than me and provided. I didn't need to work.'

'Weren't you bored?'

She laughs, showing her gums. 'But I had babies. How could I be bored?'

She makes no attempt to ask me what I did.

'You don't mind showing your gums, then?' I've had enough of this.

'Oh, I have a plate in my room but it's not very comfortable. I'm waiting to go to the dentist.'

'I'm waiting to go to bed.'

'But you've just got up and had breakfast. You've got the whole day ahead.' And she dabs at her wet mouth with her napkin.'

'Didi,' I call. 'Where's Malcolm?'

'He busy right now, Rosie. How you two gettin' on?'

'If I don't get back to my room I'll fall asleep right here.'

Her hand is on my shoulder. 'You eat like a flea, Rosie.'

'I want Janet.'

'Don't we all, Darlin'.'

TONIGHT IT'S THERE again outside my door. There's definitely muffled conversation going on. And giggling. But I think this time it might be Michael and Brenda. They're canoodling, teasing me. It'll be all her doing, smarming up to him, leading him on. I'd like to call out to shut them up but I think it will stir them to carry on.

Leaves me with a bad taste in my mouth.

Perhaps I deserve it. Perhaps everything has been my fault. Right from the beginning.

Ma's dying was my fault; I could have prevented it. Why didn't I do something or what didn't I do? Not believing Brenda was a mistake. And why couldn't Pa cope with me? What did or didn't I do that made him not love me; that made him not want me? I think it was my fault that I wasn't lovable. And of course I wasn't his. Never had been.

Perhaps Pa couldn't love. The way he'd been treated in the war. Killing the kittens; that should have warned me. Moving me to Brenda's when he knew I was happy at Margaret's. And why didn't I tell Uncle Alec what Sweaty Betty was like? And that one occasion he came to see me . . . I could have told Pa.

... I WALK in from school and he's there in the sitting room, sitting forward on the edge of the flowery armchair, holding his cap. He's rough, dirty and unshaven. I spot a tear on the shoulder of his pullover, while I'm in my white shirt and striped tie and clean shoes. Can joy and embarrassment be mixed with fear?

Aunty Bet hovers around him but not too close. She's handing him tea in a cup and saucer and he slurps it back as if he's dying of thirst and I'm thinking, Please, Pa, don't pour it in the saucer and drink from that but it's soon empty and on the small table at his side and he's on his feet, wiping his mouth as his cap falls to the floor and he's holding me.

He says, his lips near my ear, 'I'm so proud of you, Rosie in your smart uniform. And what a beauty you've become.'

And I'm thinking, Don't hold me too close, Pa, my shirt was clean on this morning.

Aunty Bet is there with us all the time in her smart dress and her hair curled and her big breasts squashed into a cotton bra that I've seen drying in the bathroom. She says, with her chin in and her lips pursed, 'Where are you living now, Frank?'

'I'm in the process of moving, Bet but I'll send you my new address.'

'Send it to me, Pa.'

His hands are on my shirt sleeves and he stoops to kiss my cheek.

'You're off then, Frank, already?'

'I've a lot to do. And thank you, Bet, for all you've done.'

He looks at me before he's out the front door . . .

I couldn't have told him the truth about Sweaty Betty, even if I'd wanted to.

LOVING MICHAEL WAS a mistake. Oh, I don't regret it but I was a fool and I let him go? Did I? Why was that?

I turn my eyes to the door. Someone has shut it. There's whispering coming underneath and the shadow of someone's feet in that haze of light from the corridor.

I could say, 'Come in,' but that's too scary. It's just like it was at home before. I'm under the slippery eiderdown in the darkness, pretending I'm not here; hiding in the shadows with the rain slashing the window and the sound of the sea roaring in the cove. I'll lie here and sweat. I probably deserve this terror.

MARGARET AND I walk towards the old house after school. There's weak sunshine and a cold wind. Our dresses are blowing against our legs and we're laughing. I am amazed that I can laugh but it's easy with her. We have the same dresses. Aunty Gracie made them; she's clever like that. She makes one for Margaret and then one for me but by then she's grumbling at the sewing machine. We're just about warm in our matching cardigans. The paths are lined with old dandelions and docks and long grasses that grow in the centre. We feel like twins but I am still confused as to how it happened so I say to Margaret, 'So, did your Pa and my Ma really love each other, I wonder?'

'I suppose they must have.'

'Brenda said it was romantic.'

'But it made Mummy unhappy when she found out. And she was already sad because Daddy was killed in the war.'

'Well, she would have been. And my ma was sad for the same reason. But I never understood how everyone knew your Pa was my Pa and I didn't.'

'They must have loved each other before the war.'

'Because don't they have to . . ?' We both giggle and blush and I don't really want to think about it and I start to feel sorry for Pa in the cottage on his own.

'Poor Pa.'

'They were both sneaky. Will he be there now, do you think, in the house? Might he be angry?'

'Let's see.'

So we creep round to the back door and I try to see through the dirty open window with the dirty grey net on a rusty wire. There's washing up piled in the sink and a saucepan on the table with a wooden spoon and the smell of old wood smoke from the grate.

'Is he there?' asks Margaret.

'I can't see him but he's been here; I know he's not in his workshop. Maybe he's in bed.'

'Are you scared?'

I bite my thumb nail. My heart pounds and I admit that I am.

'I am.'

'Try the door. I'll try the door.'

So she lifts the latch and we creep into the parlour and there on Pa's easy chair by the fire is Pretty, curled up and fast asleep.

I am so relieved that I call Pa and I hear footsteps above us and then down the stairs. Margaret backs away as he comes into the room. He has a full beard and his hair is askew and braces are holding up his baggy corduroy trousers.

'Well, well, then. And how are you two?'

I go to him and hug his thin body, overcome with pity.

'Now, now.'

I can smell his sweat. 'I'm sorry, Pa.'

'What for, Rosie. You've done nothing wrong.'

But I know I have and I cry into his shirt.

'I've been meaning to come over to Gracie's. Is she managing all right, Margaret?'

'I think so.'

I let go of him and start to stroke Pretty until she purrs.

I think he might hoof her out of his chair but he sits in the other one and pulls a filthy hanky out of his trouser pocket and blows his nose.

'I'm going to have to give up the cottage, Rosie. I've got no money coming in.'

It takes a while for this to sink in. Then I ask him what he's going to do but I know the answer. He's going away and I won't see him anymore.

'And it means you'll go to stay with your Aunty Betty and Brenda.'

Pretty jumps off the chair and walks to the cupboard looking for food.

'But I'm happy at Gracie's, Pa.' I can hardly say the words. I almost choke. Margaret slides up to me and holds my hand.

'But they're not family, Rosie and Gracie can't afford to give you the better life you deserve.'

I shout then and surprise myself. 'I don't need a better life!'

'The authorities have said that it's best for you, Lovely. You'll be taking your exam soon and it seems I have no say in the matter. And Betty is happy to have you. And you'll have Brenda.'

Bloody Brenda.

There's that time between sleeping and waking when feelings are strong, when you dream of chaos, fear or desperate longing. When you weep without tears and terror tears at you and on waking fully you are left with grief and confusion and you wonder where you are and why, let alone wondering about how you are going to cope with another day.

Michael is standing in the open doorway.

'How long have you been there?' It's my softest voice.

He comes into my room and rummages on my bedside table. 'Here, Rosie, put these on, now.'

I can see him clearer and oh, he's so handsome. 'Give me your hand,' I say and he gives it to me and I hold it in both of mine and caress it. I put it to my lips.

Then a voice. 'What's going on here, then?'

It's . . . and she's creeping in with a cup of tea.

'Just give her this moment, Elena,' he says quietly. 'She's just woken.'

'I'll move over a bit and you can squeeze in next to me. Like spoons.'

'Don't you dare, Malcolm.' Elena's hand is now at her mouth trying to stifle a laugh.

'And what's *she* laughing at?'

'Nothing, Rosie. C'mon, let's get you to drink this

cuppa.' And the cup is at my lips and I slurp the luke warm tea before it dribbles down my front.

By bedtime I'm too tired to think. What's-His-Name has been playing the accordion. Mostly jolly tunes but I'm too sleepy and too brain fogged to put in a request and Malcolm has gone somewhere - off duty, I suppose. I miss him when he's not here.

Didi takes hold of the wheelchair and I feel myself moving into the corridor and towards my room.

'Is this my room?'

'It sure is, Rosie.'

After the toilet business she's taking off my shoes, slipping off my jumper and undoing the zip at the side of my skirt before you can say Jack Somebody.

'Who'd have thought I'd be having someone undress me?'

I find it quite laughable.

'You happy tonight.' It's a statement.

'Michael tried to undress me. I had to fight him off. We laughed. But one day he succeeded because I let him.'

'You bad girl.'

We chuckle together.

'He was so gentle, undoing all those buttons and the hooks and the eyes and the stockings . . . Until I told him to stop.'

Didi says nothing.

I say nothing.

'You light as a feather, Rosie.' She takes the side off the

wheelchair and lifts me into bed. The pillows are so soft.

'Is that rain outside?'

'I think so. And wind.'

She goes to the window and pulls back one of the curtains.

'Oh, my God, Girl, it's cats and dogs out there.' She drags the curtain back into place. 'But you got no worries, 'cos you ain't got to go anywhere.'

'The sea will be rough.' I say it even though I have a vague notion that this place isn't near the sea at all. Even so, in spite of the rain and the wind and probably because of the drinking chocolate and the soft bed I let myself drift.

… I LISTEN to the wind and rain and watch as the curtains get sucked against the window. I am holding the slippery eiderdown up to my chin; it smells fousty, probably because it's filled with very old feathers. The chickens must be long dead. My knickers and vest are under it warming for the morning, for school. I think of Roger and Ian and quiet Margaret running around the playground and the school bell goes and we're lining up into a crocodile and I hold Margaret's warm hand.

But hard voices are raised downstairs and it's not Miss Noakes slapping the ruler on her thigh; it's Pa. I've not heard him quite this loud before. But even though he's loud I can't hear what he's saying. It's muffled so I sit up and listen. There's Ma's voice as well. I think it's muffled because of the wind and the rain and it frightens me. It's almost worse than the haunting. I think it is worse than the haunting . . .

Oh, it's this again. I remember this . . .

. . . There are bangs and Ma is saying animal and beast and cruel. They must think I'm asleep. Ma, at least wouldn't shout like that if she knew that I could hear. I think she must be crying. I think, if I ever have children I will never row like that. And I will never marry.

Then I hear Pa stomping up the stairs. His boots are heavy. He thumps the wall on the landing and he's in their bedroom taking off his boots and throwing them onto the floorboards. I jump at each crash. Then their bed creaks as he flops down and turns over. He must have come in from the pub. He must be drunk again or it might be because of me and I think, perhaps Brenda was right, perhaps it's because I'm a love child.

I lie there waiting for Ma but she doesn't come.

I wait and wait, biting my nails. But it's completely quiet apart from Pa's snoring. He's left the landing light on so she must be coming to bed soon.

I know the stairs will creak if I go down but not knowing is worse than knowing so I creep down to the parlour and straight away I see her face outside the window, her white face distorted by the rain.

We stare at each other for a moment until she lowers her eyes.

'Ma,' I mouth . . .

MY EYES OPEN to the one with big glasses. She's leaning over me and I can smell coffee on her breath.

'You've been shouting out, Sweetie.' Her voice is soft against my cheek. 'Are you all right?'

'I'm so scared of that door,' I admit in an equally quiet voice. Nighttime encourages quiet.

'I've just come in, Rosie and I swear that nothing is there.'

I trust her; she holds my hand so I say, 'My Ma . . .'

'I think you've been dreaming, Sweetie.'

'It was real.'

'You've been remembering, then.'

'I suppose.'

'That was a big sigh.'

'I've a lot to sigh about. I forget your name, I forget where I am, and who I am but I remember things I want to forget. Isn't that a cruel aspect of growing old?'

'Totally cruel. Do you want to talk about it? It's not good to bottle up.'

I grip her hand. 'I was responsible for my Ma's death.'

Surprisingly, she's not horrified. 'How old were you?'

'I can't remember . . . ten, maybe. It was my fault.'

'I think you need to have a cup of tea and you can tell me. Let's sit you up more.'

Then, before long she's helping me balance the cup and saucer.

'I've never liked mugs.'

'I know.'

Another one comes into my room.

'I need your help, Lottie.'

'I'll be with you when I'm done here.'

Another small act of kindness.

... SHE COMES into the parlour soaking wet and shaking and delicately places a kitchen knife in the sink.

'It's all right, Rosie,' she says.

I can see it isn't all right but I don't argue.

'Shall I get Pa?' I don't want to get him but I can't think what else to say.

She stands there, her white nightdress clinging; her hands resting on the edge of the draining board as if she's about to lose her balance.

'He's not your Pa,' she says.

And it's not the truth of it from her that upsets me; it's the fact that Brenda was right after all.

Even so, I spit, 'You're a liar!' and it comes out like hate because I'm so angry with her and because I'm cold and scared and because I need the lav and it's outside in the rain and I don't want to believe it anyway.

'The wrong man came home from the war, Rosie.'

My feet are freezing on the lino.

Ma doesn't look at me.

'Go back to bed,' she says. 'I'll come up in a minute.'

I turn and run upstairs to my room leaving her alone. I use the pot and get into bed and pull the eiderdown up to my nose, just enough to breathe. . .

. . . I left her there, with the rain pouring down outside and the wind roaring like the sea.

I left her there.

It's a beautiful morning. Sunshine through the windows and Michael places me next to the new one. She reminds me of a bird but I don't know which one. Her nose is a stubby beak like a crow but Betty and Ivy were crows and this one is not as malevolent as that two. That's a good word. Malevolent. This one can be a jackdaw; such a clever bird.

'Are you clever?

She looks startled for a second.

'I don't know. I suppose. I'm not stupid.'

She continues with her porridge and in spite of no upper teeth and a bobbing head and shaking hands she manages the spoon to mouth coordination pretty well. Albeit very slow.

'We all say that.'

'I went to grammar school,' she says.

'Ah, so did I.'

'It doesn't stop you getting Parkinson's though.'

'What's your name?'

'Pauline. It's all right, I know you're Rosie.'

'Ah, thanks for reminding me.'

Michael comes in and places his hand on my shoulder.

'This is Michael.' I hold his hand. It's warm.

'I think his name is Malcolm.'

I look around at him.

'Oh. Slip of the tongue.'

'Malcolm, take me to bed.'

The new one giggles and then Malcolm can't help but smile.

'You've just got up, Rosie.'

'But I'm so tired.'

The one in navy comes across. 'Legs this morning, Rosie.

I can't win. If it's not one vile thing it's another.

But the sun is pouring in the windows, just like . . .

IN THE MORNING Pa is dressed and at my bedroom door, his hand on the brass knob, his hair all over the place.

I blink as sunbeams squeeze through the gap in my curtains.

'Where's your Ma?' he says.

I look at him.

He says, 'She hasn't been in with you, then.'

It's more a statement than a question. He turns and rushes up the Scary Stairs.

I gasp. If he's up there then it's safe for me so I leap out of bed and follow him. He's already turning to come down again by the time I'm there and he pushes me aside in his urgency but I look in at the old suitcases, picture frames and cardboard boxes overflowing with rubbish and the cobwebs hanging from the rafters of the high ceiling.

And there, tucked under the sloping roof is Brenda's put-you-up complete with pillows and blankets, the blankets all untidy and the pillows squashed, and Ma's candlewick dressing gown on the floor.

Pa is at the back door and I follow. He opens it and the sun streams in.

Then he's at the garden gate and through it before I can get my wellies on and find my mac among the other coats.

I put it on over my nighty at a run. But I can't catch up with Pa and by the time I reach the cove he's already there, panting. I'm panting too as I stand next to him and look out to the sea and the bright sky.

But my eyes are drawn to the offshore reef like Pa's and to the swooping, shrieking sea birds.

After a short while he leans forward, his hands on his knees. His knees down. His head down.

PART THREE

If wind were to have a colour it would be grey. That cold, rough night when Ma died – it was surely grey; a grey wind, a black sky and a jagged reef out there off the cove that drew her closer and closer and there was only the flash of her white nightdress, heavy with the sea and ghostly on the eye.

I've never been a Happy Clapper or a Holy Roman. Not even a . . . but right now I could do with somebody to call on at times like this and now on top of everything else someone has stolen my glasses. I know who it is but I'll bide my time. She's bound to try it again. I'm pretty sure she's taken my polka dot nightdress as well. They won't help me look for these things either; they get me out of my room in spite of me wanting to stay in my bed so Whoever-It-Is has free access. When I've had a restless, scary night what with dreams and memories and that dreadful door, I'm always exhausted. In the morning the new one in navy says, It's your heart, Dear; try and make the most of your day. As if it might well be my last. I shall be glad when it is. Ancient Rome was good at getting out of a bad situation. Falling on swords and opening veins. If I had the guts I'd do it.

The nice one in navy saves me by bringing in the wheelchair like a chariot and aiming it at me.

'Ah! Bed!'

'Sorry, Rosie, 'fraid not. It's legs again.'

'They were only done yesterday.'

'No, it was Wednesday.'

'The days are all the same to me.'

She helps me manoeuvre into the chair and I'm soon in the treatment room, my stockings off and scabby legs exposed.

She removes the dressing. 'Slow improvement but very slow. Too slow.'

'That's all my badness coming out. On that dressing.'

'It's your heart, Rosie, It's not pumping properly; it's wearing out. I think you need the bandages on again. Stronger pressure to keep the swelling down.'

'Squeeze the life out of me. My punishment.'

'You're not being punished, My Love. We just want you to heal.'

'My Aunty Betty used to say, "You're just like you're mother, my girl; full of badness."'

'That's a horrible thing to say.' She goes to the sink and washes her hands. Always washing her hands.

'She said it was my badness when I started my

monthlies. She pretended it was a joke but there's a lot of truth in bad jokes. I had to go and live with her and her vile daughter and soon after I got there it happened, like a bad omen of things to come. Shock and terror do these things. They were always irregular, always painful. Made me faint. She had me washing my hands all the time as if I was contaminating her pristine house. And she was always cleaning the bathroom or making me clean it. I had to earn my keep.'

'I've never heard you talk so much, Rosie.'

'Don't know where it's coming from. These things spring into my mind or I dream about them. Or imagine them, perhaps . . . '

'I know it's hard for you.'

She's putting something on the ulcers but I haven't got my glasses on.

'One of these days when I've got more time, Rosie you can tell me all about your complicated life.'

'I suppose it was complicated. Perhaps that's why it's jumbled. Perhaps that's why I dream so much and worry so much.'

She's bandaging my legs. They'll be skinny soon like they were years ago. Little sticks. I never ate very much.

'I never ate very much as a child.'

'You don't now, Rosie.' She stands straight and gives me the nicest smile.

'I was happiest at Margaret's; she was my half sister.'

'I'd like to think that you're happy here too.'

'I loved Margaret . . .'

'Have you got a photo of your Pa, Margie.'

She's swinging so high and holding on so tight that her skirt is falling over her face. The sky is truly blue and I feel like we're in a warm bubble with the brilliance of the sky and the grass so green all around us.

'Oh, yes,' she says, almost upside down with her hair falling towards the ground. 'But Mum has it. She wants me to remember that I had a father and to know how lovely he was.'

I grab at the rope as she slows and she's scrabbling her daps on the grass trying to steady herself.

'You'd have thought she'd be angry with him because he and my Ma . . . And angry at me and then him being killed on top of everything.'

'Well, I don't know about that.'

'Can you show me the picture?'

'It's in Mum's bedroom.'

So I wait until we're in the house and Gracie is at her sewing machine and I nudge Margie who then asks her Mum in a whisper. 'Can Rosie see the photo of Dad?'

Gracie takes a deep breath in, squeezes a tight smile and goes upstairs. It seems ages before she comes down and we're just about to mooch off when there she is, in the parlour looking at it, her mouth fixed until she hands it to me.

'He's got a nice face' I say eventually but I don't mean it, and anyway he means nothing to me . . .

WE'RE ON THE move. Wrapped up like it's winter but there are still some flowers in the gardens as we pass. Malcolm doesn't have a warm coat, just one of those lightweight things. Elena is pushing somebody I don't recognise; some woman from another table. Malcolm's setting the pace. It's a bumpy ride.

'We're going to the park. There's a brass band.'
'I don't like brass bands.'
'We'll get you an ice cream,' shouts Elena from the rear.
'What, in this weather?'
'There will be a van; it's not that cold.'
'You could have brought . . . Thingy . . . What's-His . . .'
'He gets visitors who take him out.'
'Well, I'd just as soon be in bed.'
'Don't be such a misery, Rosie.'

It's her. I intend telling Malcolm that she's been taking things. But at least I've got my glasses back at last. She must have realised that she'd gone too far; probably a bit scared by now. Perhaps he's aware what she's doing and has persuaded her to put things back, but I've yet to see my nightdress. He's trying to protect her. That's what it is. She's got her claws into him all right and I'm sure there's something going on.

We can hear the band playing a marching tune. Cornets and trombones. The wheelchairs want to run away down the slope and Elena shrieks. Malcolm up ends mine so the back of my head is near his crotch. Oh, my, and he holds tight as it rests on the two back wheels and he laughs his head off. Michael used to laugh like that. What was his surname? Michael . . . ?

'Rosie, you're a stunner. So you are.'

I knew I was not but I loved him saying it. What I didn't know then was that he just wanted to get in my knickers. Sweaty Betty! She told me. That bitch of an aunt. She said, You're a stupid, naïve girl, Rosemary. He'll be all nice and sweet and loving until he's got what he's after. But I'm telling you, and she wagged her finger with her face close up in my face, If you let him make you pregnant you'll be out of this house, and Toute Suite, as if she was an expert in French but I knew she wasn't. I almost said, You stupid cunt of a woman; that's what I want, can't you see? I want him in my knickers and I want to get out of this house. And I was able to say that word because I'd heard Pa say it on one occasion when he'd come home from the pub in a rage and Ma was stunned like he'd slapped her because she stood there with her mouth open and then she began to cry and I thought it must be the worst word you could say to somebody.

I wonder if Malcolm has been in Elena's knickers? I bet he has. Good healthy young male.

The band is applauded by all the people hanging around, some in folding chairs, some on benches. All these people. All these pigeons strutting about, pecking at each other, shitting on each other, and all of them wishing they were doves like the beautiful minority. Malcolm can be a seagull, a superior bird with that wide wingspan. Swooping down and around the offshore reef, those black rocks jutting up out of the sea like a jagged-backed sea monster.

IT SEEMED AS if I'd only been at Margaret's a short time when Sweaty Betty and Aunty Vi came knocking at the door.

I knew something was up as soon as Pa arrived as well. He was all dishevelled and grubby. Dirty fingernails on his big hands and he wrapped his arms around me like a vice in front of all of them in the hallway. Margie started playing with her hair and both the aunties were standing there tight lipped and tidy.

'Rosemary, leave your father alone,' says Vi, 'You'll suffocate him.'

And Betty says, 'He's not her father, Ivy,' as if she needed reminding.

It seems to me that the whole world knows more than I do. But he's still the only Pa I've ever known and I take in his bad smell and I don't mind because I can't help thinking that I'll never see him again and that he doesn't really want what's about to happen, any more than me.

'Frank, for goodness sake,' says Vi, like, stop the emotional clap trap; be a man.

He releases me, reluctantly I think but instantly stands tall and stares at the two witches with a dislike I admire. Then he puts his hand in his top jacket pocket and puts something onto my palm. He squeezes my fingers over it until Betty says, 'Rosemary, get your things together, you're coming with us now. And no fussing, it's all organized.'

'And your Aunty Bet has arranged a place for you at the grammar school.'

'You're a very lucky girl to have the opportunity.'

'But it was Rosie who passed the exam, Vi,' says Gracie, coming in from the kitchen.

She's got cups of tea on a tray and they leave me alone as they move into the front room, sit in comfy chairs and drink from flowery cups.

Margie holds my hand.

'Go on, you two. Up the stairs,' says Gracie in a soft voice. 'I've put a suitcase in your room. Help Rosie pack, Margaret.' She gives a small push on our backs and I start to feel sick but am determined not to cry.

When I come down the stairs with the suitcase that's half empty Pa has gone and I feel utterly alone.

'Let's get on with this then,' says Vi, and she takes the case and turns to the door.

I look at Margie who is hugged up next to her Ma and I am ushered outside to a black taxi and am in it before you can say anything. I have never been in a taxi. I force myself not to look back so I open my fingers. He's given me Ma's wedding ring.

THAT BITCH OF a girl with the fancy accent is rummaging in my bedside cabinet. She thinks I don't know what she's up to. She takes me for a fool but I can see what she's doing. Right under my eyes. She's looking for my jewellery.

'You won't find any,' I mutter.

'Any what?'

She's got such a nerve.

'Jewellery.' Now she's aware that I know.

'I didn't know you had jewellery, Rosie.'

She thinks she's smart. 'I have a ring in there that's important to me.'

'Well, it should be in the safe. We should have picked it up when you arrived. Shall I look for it?'

Now, here's a conundrum. Do I let her look for it and find it? But she'll then wait for her opportunity to take it. Or do I let her look and not find it because she's got it hidden away somewhere already? And I won't be able to accuse her because no-one knows I have it anyway.

'What are you rummaging for? You won't find the ring.'

Ha! That's a good manoeuvre.

She stands at the side of the bed. 'I'm looking for your polka dot nightdress. Haven't seen it for a while.'

You may look confused, my girl but you don't fool me. 'Someone (and that's someone with a capital S) has stolen it.'

She's putting on that look again. 'Now, why would Anyone (with a capital A) want to steal your nightdress?'

'You tell me.'

'You'll have to put on your pink one.' She's getting snakey now.

'Never liked pink. Ever.

I'm eventually trundled into the dining room.

'See you've found your glasses,' says What's-Her-Name.

'See you've found your teeth.'

I want Janet. She's not Janet.

How is it that something as innocuous as a door can become such a thing of horror?

A simple panelled white door with brass effect furniture. The one at home had a knob that wobbled. This one has a handle that's pulled down. A typical bad choice because how can you open it with arthritic hands? Elena, the magpie always leaves it ajar which is kind of her, considering.

Michael suddenly appears; he's peeping around it with that captivating smile. But it's not until he's fully in my room that I realise it's Malcolm.

'Ah, my darlin' Rosie, have you had a good lie on the bed, now? Is it doin' those legs any good? Increasin' the blood flow?

'You increase my blood flow, Malcolm, just like Michael did way back. Come closer and let me touch you.'

He sidles up and I take his hand, touch his wrist where the hairs are and he lets me caress his arm.

'Now, why didn't you marry that Michael, Rosie, when you loved him so?'

'It was because of Brenda and her cunt of a mother.'

'Rosemary Cooper!' It's Didi coming in. 'You goin' to have your mouth washed out with soap good and proper.'

'Brenda's mother, the beast called Betty said that to me many times but she never did it. She said I lied all the time but I didn't. It was Brenda.'

I've said too much and remembered too much. Somebody will be scratching that door tonight because I've stirred things up again . . .

BE CAREFUL WHAT or who you love and never love too much or life will come along and slap your face.

I knew the dream would end badly as soon as I saw the solitary figure at the end of the avenue of lime trees. I could have been looking into a kaleidoscope. Leaves and branches all the way round making a tunnel and the faraway man doing semaphore in the small circle of light at the end, his back against the sun. And me without my glasses, straining to see. Then the awful realisation that it's Michael because I recognise his shape and he's waving at me; not waving like he wants me to rush to him or that he's simply trying to attract my attention but waving goodbye in the serious slowness that happens in dreams. My heart is being torn out. My pound of flesh taken.

SOMEONE HAS LEFT a tap running. There's a slow, slopping sound somewhere. I've not the strength to get out of bed on my own any more or I'd be there hunting out the source. There's a bell here if I can find it. Or I could yell. But yelling in the dark in the middle of the night is something I've never been able to do. The past comes back to me and I'm staring at the door. There's no scratching, no breathing and no knocking but my eyes drift down in the darkness and I can vaguely see a glint of light on something moving and I can see that it's water. It's water seeping under the door very slowly and it's not just the sound of it but it's the smell. The salt and the seaweed and the dead fish.

In the morning one of them is saying, Good morning, Rosie. Cup of tea? I try to open my mouth to reply but nothing comes out. I try again but I can't move at all.

The teacup is placed on my bedside cabinet and someone's face is at my face calling my name. Once, twice, three times. I think they find the bell because someone else comes in, then the nice one in navy and . . .

They must have mopped up the water and I didn't notice.

Perhaps this is how Janet felt.

'Shall I ring for Dr Pearce?'

'Where's the Sphyg?'

'TIA? Do you think?'

'CVA, more like.'

'Aspirin? Sister?'

'She's doing the vitals.'

'BP raised. Ring Dr Pearce.'

'It might be a bleed.'

'Rosie. Can you speak? Can you blink? Can you lift your arms?'

'Janet had a bleed.'

'All of you out! Now! Malcolm, you stay with me. Out! All of you!'

'Rosie, darlin', look at me.'

I'll look at him any day. Oh, Michael. Such green eyes. Let me look at you. Let me . . .

'She's lookin' at me, so, she is. Jesus, Mary and Joseph.'

I want to laugh but I leave the laughing to Mmma . . . .

.

Pansy Pearce looks me over and considers. 'Is there a DNR, Sister?'

She glances my way then ushers him to the doorway.

I can still hear the . . . cconver. . . . .

'Her cousin has signed one with her. So, yes.'

'I think we just start aspirin and wait and see.'

'No MRI?'

'Let's wait and see.'

So I could bleed to death. Ha! Exsanguin . . . That will do me. Rivers of blood, Enoch. Perhaps, now they'll let me rest in bed.

Oh, it's Bloody Brenda again. And me, helpless.

'I'm sorry to see you like this, Rosie.'

She stoops with a kiss for the top of my head. 'But I think they're doing the right thing by not putting you through all those investigations. Lorna's gone for a coffee. Think it'll be better that it's just you and me. I need to get down to the nitty gritty, need to say sorry, ask for your forgiveness. Well, on Mummy's behalf, really. She's the one who needs forgiveness. I know she was unkind to you and Daddy didn't know half of it. Always playing golf or whatever. I did tell him once . . .'

Once.

'. . . about the cupboard business and he said he'd speak to Mummy. I couldn't influence her. I was always at work doing my apprenticeship. Remember coming into the salon after school and you'd be my model? You always went home looking glamorous. All that backcombing and bouffant; no wonder Michael wanted you. I think Declan did as well but Michael had the guts to do something about it at the time. Swept you off your feet, didn't he? But it was you decided on college. You risked losing him. It wasn't my fault. And in spite of Mummy failing you it was she who set up the fund to pay for your care, should you ever need it. Wrote it into her will. I'm the one who's seen it through, though. She always felt guilty. You didn't know that, did you? And I've suffered grief as well as you. Mummy dying. You knew that Michael . . . No I won't go there, I won't be cruel like Mummy was and I admit she was. Cruel, at times.'

She's getting out her fucking hanky!

'But I often wondered how far you went with Michael. You were such a timid thing of a girl and I admit I was jealous.'

That's it. Wipe your fucking eyes and your fucking nose.

'I'm not admitting to anything, mind. It wasn't my fault. These things happen in life. I never encouraged him.'

Oh, liar, liar, house on fire.

'Ah! Brenda, is it?' Malcolm walks in the room that suddenly feels overcrowded and stifling. I need my inhaler. 'Tryin' to cheer our sweet Rosie up?'

'I think she's beyond cheering up.'

'Give me a minute and let me look in her eyes; I can tell if she's happy or not.'

Benda looks down her nose at Malcolm. She has the ability to do that even from a sitting position. 'And you are?' she asks.

'Now, Rosie. Listen.' He's lowered his voice just enough to direct it straight into my ear but loud enough for Brenda to hear. 'D'ye want me to get tea and cake for your lovely cousin here or do you want me to tell her to piss off?'

'Ppp . . .'

'She wants you to go home, now if you don't mind. She's very tired.'

Tail between her legs. Ha!

She's gathering up her stuff, bag, stick and scarf and he's escorting her out to the main corridor and the front door being ever so polite. She'll sit outside on the bench and keep dropping her stick and she'll try to contact Lorna on her mobile, her hand shaking.

Then he's back in the doorway, beaming.

I attempt a smile. It'll be crooked, no doubt but he descrves a smile.

'Mmmalcolm . . .

'Rosie,' he holds my hand and shakes his head slowly in what looks like wonder. He says, 'I love you.'

BUT *SHE,* BRENDA has left me discombobulated again. Dr Something comes in with the new one in navy. I guess she's not so new now but she loves having that sphyg thing round her neck and a file under her arm, looking important.

All this endless company and they wonder why I'm so tired all the time.

'She's doing well, Doctor. Speech is coming back rapidly now. You were right to 'wait and see'.'

'Mmm. Can you tell me what month we're in, Rosemary?'

'N . . .'

'Time of the year?'

'N . . o.'

'Are you trying to say November or No, Dear.'

If I look at them with a blank stare they might go away.

'Look out of the window, Rosie. What do you see?'

There's no let up. Hm. The trees are changing colour from green to that wonderful golden yellow and bronze. Solitary falling leaves and I'm in amongst them with Michael, scuffing them up, my hand in his.

'Does that ring any bells for you?'

'I need time to . . .' Michael is going to drift from me again if I'm not careful. Stay with me. Just a little longer. We can kiss, his hands on my hips, his face close to mine. Oh. The sun through the trees, the autumn leaves drift by my . . . 'It's Autumn.'

'Well done.'

'Do I get a st . . .icker?'

'And how are the legs, Sister?'

'No change.'

'Or a paper h . . ?

'Mmm. Think she can sit out for a little. Feet up, of course. Breathing?'

'We're coping, Doctor.'

We?

'Appetite?'

Who's he asking? Appetite for what? That slop from the

kitchen? I've never had an appetite. All my life. Slop in the cottage, slightly better slop at Margie's, slop at Betty's (and not much of it, thank God. She was tight with . . .) and slop at . . . I catch a head shake from The New One.

'We do try to give her a varied diet but there's no enthusiasm.'

'Ok, that will do for today. Keep smiling, Rosie.' He pats my hand like he'd pat a dog but he doesn't look at me. Neither does she.

'Where's Malcolm?'

It's Elena. Looks like she's had a good slapping, face all puffy and pink. She shrugs and blows into a tissue. 'He has been – I think the word is, reprimanded. Could be suspended if it goes any further. Your cousin has made a complaint. She said that he told her to piss off.'

'No.' I try to suppress a smile as I shake my head. Silly me; don't do that; I might aggravate the old brain. The bleeding or the clots. Not that I care, but I've got things to sort out in my head first.

'They won't accept it. According to them you were clearly not speaking properly at the time. They say that Malcolm eggs you on; is that the right word, what I'm saying? They say he behaves improperly with you.'

'Who's "they"?'

'You know. The top dogs.'

'I want the nice one in navy.'

'Jennifer?'

'Yes, her.'

'The complaint will go to the owners of the home unless he apologises.'

He'll find that difficult, I'm sure but Brenda will love it. The grovelling.

Elena starts to sniff and rips the tissues out of the box on my bedside table one by one.

'I'm sorry, Rosie.'

Is she grovelling to me? Ah, the ring.

'Have you got my ring?

'What? What ring are you talking about?'

'It doesn't matter.' What does anything matter any more? 'I guess it doesn't matter any more.'

She doesn't show any recognition. Too young. But Michael and I would sing it together in the woods, not concentrating on the lyrics; until later of course when Brenda got her teeth into him. Like her with her runny nose getting her teeth into Malcolm.

She flounces out and I turn with difficulty and stretch my arm between the bars on the side of my bed. Cot sides. Might as well be in jail. But I manage to reach the drawer of the bedside cupboard. I throw stuff out onto the bed but mostly it slides off the duvet and onto the floor: hairbrush, empty purse, handkerchief, perfume, lippy. Not much for all my years.

What was the point of all that, though? Was I looking for anything in particular?

I might as well not be here. This room the size of a hanky. That enormous door with its secrets and me, shrivelling into nothing, drifting into the shadows again, pushed into cupboards; told to, Get to bed, Rosemary, I need some peace and quiet. And there's Michael on the lawn outside my window throwing stones, calling out just like Romeo. . .

'*Rosie!*' in a loud whisper.

I'm giggling at the window as I push the sash upwards.

'*I'm comin' in that feckin' window, now. Up the feckin' drain pipe.*' And he's feeling with his feet and holding on and his jacket's flapping and his hair's flying and he's hanging over the window ledge stifling a laugh until he's on my bedroom floor in quiet hysterics.

'Rosemary?' It's Uncle Alec calling from the bottom of the stairs. 'Are you all right up there?'

'I'm fine, Uncle, Ta. Been sorting my books. Getting ready for the 'off' next week.'

'Tell her to put the light out and get to sleep.'

'It's all right, Bet. She's going to.'

'*So, what'll happen if they find I'm here, then?*' He's been drinking and his arms are around me already, slipping my dressing gown off my shoulders and he's laughing and whispering in my ear.

'Be quiet, Michael,' I plead.

'*I'm getting' in your bed, now, Darlin'. Come on, it'll be grand.*' He shrugs off his jacket and shoes, lifts the blankets and gets in and I join him really fearful of what we might do but we're lying together, touching and kissing, his hands wandering . . . under my nighty . . .

'Rosie!'

And Michael's gone.

'What's going on here, Rosie Girl?'

'Nothing's going on. What's likely to 'go on' here in this cage?'

'I'm talkin' about all this mess on the floor.'

Then her backside is in the air and she's picking up the bits and pieces.

'Oh, my God, I can't do this sort of bendin' any more.'

'I'm sorry, Didi.'

There was a lot going on when Michael was in my bed…

… The laughing calms down and his body is close to mine but we are so hot in spite of the cold weather that he throws the blankets back and we're under the sheet and he's undoing his shirt buttons and his fly buttons.

'Get yer kit off, Rosie, my love. Let me see your soft white skin and your little beaver, there.'

But I can smell the beer and in spite of me wanting him I'm overwhelmed with guilty memories – Aunty Bet saying to me, Your mother has let us all down, Rosemary, and Pa staggering home from the pub and the fear of pregnancy like Ma must have felt and the fear of Aunty's wrath so I push him away and the sheet gets in a mess but he doesn't take me seriously and his laughing gets louder as the door opens and Brenda is there, eyes wide open and mouth covered with her hand so I can't see if she's sniggering or about to turn and call for Sweaty Betty.

I swing my feet onto the floor and pull my nightdress down. 'You didn't knock,' I say trying to appear superior.

Brenda looks at Michael who is still in bed, his hands

behind his head looking soppy and then she looks at me.

'Ah do declare, Miss Rosemary,' she says in her Scarlett O'Hara voice, 'You ain't nothin' but a prick teaser.' She looks at Michael and they smirk together and I feel the fool yet again as he gets out of bed, picks up his shoes and jacket and follows her out of my room. They creep down the stairs like mice, like conspirators and I'm out of the picture altogether. She's got him in the palm of her hand now, all right.

ANDY IS UNPACKING his accordion. 'Evening, Ladies and Gents. Let's have your requests.'

'I don't want any more of those Irish songs, thank you. And I'm sorry but I've forgotten your name.'

'Andy,' fills in Pauline. 'His name is Andy.'

'I know that.'

'So why the rejection of the Irish music?'

'I have my reasons.'

'Have you gone off Malcolm, then? Has he upset you?' She starts slurping up her soup. Some falls into her pelican bib.

'Don't talk rubbish.'

'I hear he's back next week. Had a few days off. Apologising.'

'You're a gossip monger.'

'It's not gossip; it's a fact. He spoke out of turn to a visitor. Elena has been bereft.'

'Elena is soppy about him but it's not recip . . .recip . . . This sandwich is tasteless.'

'What's in it? '

'God knows. She's got him in the palm of her hand, sure enough. I'm going to tell him that she's a scheming little thief.'

'Thief?'

'She's taken things from my locker. I shall tell him and see what he says. If he wants to protect her I'll know how far it's gone.'

'Freda?' This one is calling her over but Freda can't move because she's stuck in her chair.

'She can't get out of that chair, Silly. And she wouldn't know if things have gone missing or not. Have you seen my mother's wedding ring?'

'Have you been wearing it?'

'I have never, ever worn a ring.'

Andy is starting up his . . . squeeze thing. I've heard that tune before. Freda is joining in. Oh, God.

LAST NIGHT THERE was gentle tapping on my door. I knew it hadn't gone away. I knew it would be back at some point. Something stirs it up. There's a small light on the patio that I can just catch a glimpse of through the gap in my curtains but otherwise it's black out there and it's past midnight black. When I think the tapping has finished for the night and I feel really tired it decides to try again. Tap, tap, tap. Hardly loud enough to hear but I know it's there.

In the morning, of course I'm exhausted and when Malcolm comes in and he says, Morning, Rosie, I've forgotten he's been away until he reminds me and it's such a relief to see him again that my fear from the night disappears for a while.

'What have you been up to then, Rosie? Stirrin' things up with Pauline and Arthur?'

'I don't know what you mean, you lovely man. I'm just overjoyed to see you. It's just that Elena has been knocking my door again in the night.'

'Elena doesn't do it, Rosie, you know that well enough. I think it's your memories of the past.'

'Memories? Outside my door? I don't know what you're saying.'

'Perhaps I should say, ghosts of the past. But I don't want you scared, now.'

I'm silenced with this revelation, 'Ghosts of the past'? I was a child back then; I didn't have a past. So I drift back to the dead. There's Ma and there's Pa. Both gone. There's Aunty Bet and Uncle Alec. There's Margaret and Gracie and my real Pa . . . His name has gone. And there's Aunty Vi, nasty woman.

And there's Michael. Is he dead? Has he gone too?

'There, now, Rosie. I've made you cry. Here, take this and wipe those brown eyes. Let's see them glow and crinkle. C'mon, I'll get you up for breakfast and see if you can manage more than a spoonful of cornflakes this mornin'.'

MICHAEL. The end of that first happy term and we are into the New Year of . . . nineteen-fifty . . . and hearing Buddy Holly on the wireless and the meaning of the words are in my head, so much so that in the cold and windy woods our stilted laughter can't help but make me wonder what Brenda has been up to. We kiss and I tell him I love him but he doesn't sweep me up in his arms and twirl me round, he says, I love you too. But 'Rosie' is not at the end of his sentence, his words drift around the bare branches and the ivy and our hallowed place is no longer hallowed to me. I am surprised that it isn't raining by now; it would be very apt. The sky is darkening and ominous and I can sense that it will rain but there's no urgency to get back to Betty's. I find myself unable to question him. I am unable to speak naturally. I look for his hand and it's there but not there. Our fingers interlock.

'Rosie.'

He says my name now as if he wants to start a conversation that's difficult but I stop him. I'm not ready for it.

'Don't.'

He looks at me sideways and says nothing.

It's like the song; it's raining in my heart.

The Nice One comes into my room after my lie down in the afternoon. There's a gale outside and leaves are blowing around my window. It's so cosy under the duvet.

'Sorry to disturb you, Rosie. Do you want to get up?'

'No.'

She drops the cot side, pulls up a chair and sits down. I've never seen her sit before.

'Would you like me to do your nails?' She takes my hand. 'Your fingers are cold.' So she warms them in hers until she's ready.

She cuts them; must have anticipated this because she has nail clippers, and a thingy board and hand cream plonked on my bedside table.

'Tell me about your young years, Rosie. Unless it upsets you, of course.'

'Why should it upset me?'

'I can't imagine that you have always been curmudgeonly.'

'Ha, that's a good word.'

'You like words.' It's a statement.

'I was a teacher. Primary school. Lovely boys and girls. I'd read to them. Brenda wasn't educated.'

'Your cousin.' Another statement.

'And yet she had more get up and go than me.'

'Oh?'

'She stole Michael from me. I don't blame him. He appeared so self assured but he couldn't resist her, I suppose. She was so glamorous . . .'

MICHAEL IS THERE in the background, in Betty's house, in the front room looking sheepish and Brenda is in front of me with a smirk that he can't see. I think he's almost cowering, afraid of what she might say.

'Come out with it, Brenda.' I've found inner strength from somewhere.

'Ah do declare, Miss Cooper . . .

'Stop it. Stop being stupid and tell me.' I look around her and he's blushing. He's actually blushing.

He says, 'Rosie, I'm sorry.'

'You weren't here, Miss Cooper. You were away teaching those tiny boys and girls.' She's a child now, addressing me . . .

'Go on, Rosie.' It's Jennifer, the kind one.

'I dream about him . . .'

Sure, Rosie It's not going to work. And I know you have to leave.' and there's me fighting through the dream crowd that prevents him coming after me and stopping me and he's gone to where people go to in the dream world . . .

'Tell me about your mother and father.'

'Oh, I can't do that.'

'They must have loved you?'

'No idea.'

'What changed after your father came home from the war?'

'He wasn't my pa after all.

'I didn't know that.'

'The wrong man came home from the war. So they say.'

She's looking confused and I know I'm confused. She starts using that thing, that board, the file.

'I thought it was all sorted in my head but now I wonder about things.'

'It's good to talk.' She's massaging my hands with some beautiful smelling cream. It's hypnotising.

'You know what's so rotten about being old? If you're

married one of you is bound to die and leave the other alone and if you stay single you're alone anyway and may never get touched in a loving way ever again. And being eighteen now is nothing like it was in my day.'

'And you have regrets?'

'Oh, yes.'

'You never had children?'

'I had thirty children in my classroom every day. I didn't need more. And besides I had my chance and I messed it up.'

'You said a while ago that you were responsible for your mother's death?'

'Is that a question?'

'I suppose it is. I mean that's one hell of an admission.'

'I am totally to blame. I could have done so much. Why didn't I . . ?

'Sister!' It's . . . opening the door and poking her head round.'

'Knock, Ola, before you barge in!'

'Sorry, Sister, but can I have the keys for Malcolm? Freda needs her medication.'

She gets up from the chair and straightens her back.

'I'm coming now! Let's continue this conversation another time, Rosie. I think it's important that we do.'

She picks up her bits and pieces and leaves just when I might have told her so much more. And maybe she's right. Maybe the ghosts out there will go away if I can exor . . .

They don't keep on to me any more about getting up. It's a relief. It's a relief to be able to drift in peace. I imagine it might be like this if I were coming in and out of consciousness.

That man. My real pa. I'll never now know what he was like. Why didn't I ask?

And Pa. I never understood what he went through until later when I started devouring books with a vengeance. And what happened to him? He came to see me at Betty's. Once. He said he was going somewhere. Maybe Liverpool? Manchester? Somewhere. He sent me an address on a scruffy piece of paper and I wrote to him. How many times did I write? But I never had a reply. How hard did I try to find him? Why didn't I try harder?

And Ma. How cruel I was.

The something of the falling wren . . . ? or was it a falling sparrow? Think. The readiness is all. Ma was that wren but her death wasn't expected so soon; she wasn't ready. I could have saved her. I could have been kind and put my arms around her. I could have told her I loved her. I could have called Pa. But at that moment I hated her as she stood in the kitchen by the sink and left me wondering if the knife was for Pa or for her. Calling her a liar . . . Saying I hated her. Did I really say that?

'You're a liar', I spit. And I'm angry. I'm angry because I'm scared and I'm angry because Pa is not my real pa and it's her fault. I'm cold and I need a wee, so much so that I race upstairs to the pot and I don't think of waking Pa or of going downstairs again to see if she's all right. I crawl into bed under the slippery eiderdown and rough blankets and I shiver and feel sorry for myself.

And I go to sleep.

Ma is under the earth. They are dropping handfuls of soil on top of the coffin, the noise of it louder than you'd imagine it would be but it's a calm sunny day, the sky is streaked with blues and yellows and soft clouds and the sea birds are soaring but not screeching. I will never forget the screeching on that terrible day. They screeched at me and at Pa. But kept silent for the wren.

Ma is under the earth and I put her there. The guilt is overwhelming and the police are on their way, delayed perhaps by the roaring wind. Or is it the sea? It's the waves crashing and the pebbles dragging but it's not the fear of capture that's scaring me, it's the fear of seeing her body when it's dragged out of the grave and it will be pulled out covered in wet mud, manhandled and left on the wet grass. Oh, wake up, wake up. I am soaking in the sea spray and sweat . . .

'Malcolm, you must have a word with Elena. She's taken all my photographs.'

'Where were they, Rosie?'

'In there. Wherever else might they be?' and I'm

throwing my arms around, trying to locate the bedside locker.

'Stop that, now, Lovely, it's makin' you cough like Billy-O.'

'I don't want that bloody thing, that . . . whatever it's called. It's that that makes me cough.'

'It's the nebuliser, Rosie. Now take it. There's a good girl.'

'I don't want that thing on my face.'

'Now, stop this flailing around, Darlin'.'

'You all right there, Malcolm?'

'She won't take it, Sister.'

'We'll get the oxygen. I'll ring Dr Pearce.'

'Do you think I need a vicar then, Sister? Or a . . . ?

'Stop it, Rosie, now, you're becoming troublesome, so you are.'

'A curate will do. Absolve me of my sins.'

'You've done nothing sinful, My Dear.'

Oh, God, it's the other one.

'Jane, phone Graham and ask him to write up oxygen for Rosie. Now, please.'

'Get a cylinder from storage, Malcolm. And make sure it's full.'

Malcolm's on a mission now all right.

'And in date, Malcolm!' she calls after him.

'So do I need the last rites, Sister?'

'YOU'VE NEVER HAD photographs in your locker, Rosie. And why accuse me?

'I want the photo of my Pa.'

'I know nothing about it.' Her face is crumpling. Oh, for God's sake.

'Stop being a softy. What's your name? And tell Malcolm I'd like to see him. *Please*. And ring Mr Eastwood and tell him I'd love to do a face thingy with him on one of your contraptions.'

'You're getting ridiculous and demanding, Rosie. You're worse than ever.'

'Hey, hey, what's going on now? Sure, I don't like all this upset.'

'She's accusing me of . . .'

'Elena, my sweet, she is not herself. Make allowances. She's a seriously ill lady.'

And right there, in *my* room they wrap their arms about each other and he kisses her. He pecks her forehead and her nose and her generous mouth. I knew it. She's got her claws into him all right.

'What's your real name, Elena? Is it Brenda?'

I'm as jealous as hell.

THERE'S THAT PLASTIC thing over my face.

'Stop fighting it, Rosie; it'll help you breathe.'

'It's fresh air I need.'

But they're not listening to me or can't hear me because I'm talking into this mask. I want it *off*.

'All right, Rosie. Let's just hold it in front of her face for a while. Is that better?'

'It's making me cough.'

'I think the nebuliser would be better.'
'Yes.'
'Let's get Graham in here.'

'While you're on the phone . . .' They're all looking at me. Get a line through to Clint. He'll understand an . . . oldies need. Bet he's still got a sex drive. Oh, I could make up for lost time with him. And a fuck or two could see me out . . . without all these wires and plastic. I don't do plastic. Oh, Michael, where are you?

There's a child in my room. A boy. He's pointing at me, probably looking at the mask on my face.

There's also a woman. She's bundled up in a bobble hat and matching scarf. She starts to peel the scarf off. 'So good to see you again, Rosie,'

'Better than seeing me in a coffin, I suppose.'

I don't know who the hell she is. The boy is fresh faced and smiling just like some of the children in my class. I can see him looking at my bed. He's wanting to get up onto it.

I pull off the mask. 'It's too high for you. But if you do manage it they'll be here soon enough to drag you off.'

She's undoing the buttons on her coat, shrugging out of it and sitting herself down in the chair.

'What's the boy's name?'
'Finn.'
'Now that rings a bell. Finn, come closer so I can see you. Have we met before?'

'I don't think so, Granny.'

That's a new one. Granny.

'You can call her Granny if you wish, Finn , but I'm your real one.'

'I don't think I know you.'

'Finn, go to Rosie's locker and get the glasses for her.'

He helps me to put them on. His small hands are quite cold. I try to warm them in mine but he pulls away.

'I'm Lorna. Brenda's daughter.'

'Really? You've aged.'

I shouldn't have said that but she chuckles and says, 'I am in my sixties, Rosie and Finn is my Liam's son.

I'm trying to get my head round all this information when she says, 'I'm bringing sad news, Rosie.'

'Oh, I understand sad; it's followed me all my life.'

'Mummy died a few weeks ago. She was eighty-seven. I couldn't come any sooner; there's been so much to do.'

'Another one bites the dust, then. In all honesty I don't care. I know she was your mother but . . .'

She rummages around in her bag. 'I've brought you this,' and she hands over a gold ring.

'Is this my mother's ring?'

'Shall I put it on your finger, Granny Rosie?'

'Mmmm. Does it fit?'

'It fits perfectly.'

'So I can go to the ball tonight and meet the Prince. And marry the prince.'

'You're thinking of a glass slipper,' and he laughs out loud.

'Who had it, Lorna?'

'My Granny Betty kept it safe for you; Mummy always said that Betty thought you would lose it.'

'I could do nothing right according to her. I know she was your grandmother but she was a hateful person. Sweaty Betty.'

The boy shouts with laughter.

'Sweaty Betty, on the jetty. Full of sin, push her in; make her wetty.'

Oh, how lovely to hear the boy's laughter.

'You're a dear boy. Come here and let me look at your eyes.'

His face is very close to mine. 'You have green eyes, Michael.'

He finds that hilarious too. 'I'm not Michael. He was my great granddad.'

Did I know that?

'Rosie Sweet, it's you I love but I've been such a fool.'

'I'M SORRY ROSIE,' says Brenda.

I start to sing, 'I'm sorry, so sorry, that I was such a . . . How apt is that, Brenda? You wanted him and you got him. You can keep him.'

The suitcase I arrived with is heavier this time and I drag it down the stairs, bump, bump, bump but I don't have anything of Michael's to take with me.

And I don't want anything.

'I'm not coming back ever again, Aunty Bet.' I'm heartbroken.

'Oh, I think you will, you ungrateful girl.'

'Did they marry?' I ask.

'No. Mummy was furious but he did stay with her for a few years. But then he died of cancer.' He was thirty-two.

My heart thumps away in my chest. I'm really conscious of it. I think it's going to stop. Did I really think that he might still be alive?

'I've forgotten what he looked like.'

'Here,' and she scratches around in her bag. Hands me a photograph from a wallet. 'When I was born. With Mummy and Michael.'

Ohhhhhhh . . .

Oh . . .

There's a huge storm. It must be dusk by now and rain is lashing the window. They will be in here soon to pull the curtains but I don't mind watching the rain. It's comforting in its continuity. It will be lashing down at the cove right now and the breakers will be breaking over the wet sand and the pebbles and the shells and the sea weed. Bladderwrack and sugar kelp and . . . stretching along the coast for miles and miles . . . and . . . the barbed wire will be long gone.

And Pa is here, my tiny hand in his rough hand and we look out to the horizon and smell the salt spray and he says, 'The sea is full of salt. Taste it on your lips.' I look up at him and grasp hard on his hand. Don't ever go away again, Pa. I think. Don't leave me.

Then the sun comes out from its hiding place and Margie is there waving from the sand dunes and calling out. I turn and call to her to come but she's not waving to say, hello, she's waving to say, goodbye and I watch as she disappears through the gorse and grasses. I can hear her shouting and playing with Ian Penny and Roger . . . And Veronica with her wet knickers. Oh, we were cruel. All pigeons wishing we were doves. And Miss Noakes waving her ruler about, threatening the boys, but with a glint in her eyes and always an arm round our shoulders; she lets us know we're special without her having to say a word.

And there's Michael and Malcolm standing together at the edge of the sea, their trouser legs rolled up and their faces turned towards the sun, laughing.

And here am I watching for water babies, hoping one might pop into the real world.

Ma, where are you?

THERE'S DARK AND there's dark, dark and tonight it's dark, dark. I'm having trouble thinking and breathing. They'll be in here soon to put that thing on my face. Not that it does any good.

There's a special providence in the fall of a . . . cuckoo. Ha!

THE STORM HAS settled. It's dead quiet.

So why have I woken? Of course . . . it's those two, Elena and Malcolm, full of fun and besotted with each other. They've been hanging around outside my door, tapping. They think it's a great game and I know and accept that I really am one penny less than a shilling now.

Tap, tap.

They'll come barging in any minute. Well, I'll tell them that I don't care one jot what's outside that door anymore.

There's a lamp on my locker but I can't remember where the switch is. It might be on the cable or on the brass bit under the bulb. I fiddle with the shade but my hands are shaking and the lamp topples to the floor.

That will bring them in. Even if it's not them outside they'll be here in two shakes. I'm holding my breath when it's there again. Tap, tap, tap. A little louder but still tentative.

Then for some reason I think of Ma and picture her sitting at the bottom of the Scary Stairs outside my bedroom door, slowly rocking, her arms clasped around herself. I wonder why I never called her in? All those nights. Afraid to disturb me. I could have called her in.

'Ma,' I whisper now, 'come in.' I manage to turn on my side. 'Ma. Push the door open and come in.'

The door opens as I knew it would. A few inches but enough for her to slip through because she's stick thin like me. She crawls into the bed beside me and her skin is damp like when you've been standing in the salt wind for ages and her hair is matted like she's been in the sea but the two of us share the warmth of my nest; the cuckoo and the wren, my wing around her, speaking into her ear that's like a sea shell.

'I'm sorry, Ma.' and I tell her how much I love her and it's

        oh

                so

Printed in Dunstable, United Kingdom